D1518291

BEHIND THE

Lens

USA *TODAY* bestselling author

RENEE HARLESS

BEHIND THE

Lens

Everything isn't always what it seems. . . behind the lens.

From drug cartels to classified information, Cliff knows a thing or two about secrets. As a part of an underground government reconnaissance team, he's seen it all. Until his latest mission.

Making mistakes isn't an option for people like Alexis. From group homes to moving around with the FBI, her feet never hit solid ground. One wrong move and suddenly her life isn't just in chaos— it's in jeopardy. Running for her life lands her in the arms of the first and only man ever to give her a reason to stay.

It's been two years since he's seen her, but it only takes him a split second to know that this time she's not getting away.

Cliff puts his training to use and his life on the line to protect Alexis. . . and make her his.

Prologue

A round him, the air grew thick and heavy as he settled into place. Blades of the wheat brushed against the material of his pants, the grains tickled his forearms as he crouched onto the ground. Within the dense fog, a sheen of mist coated his skin and caused a shiver to travel down his spine. Fall weighed heavy in the air, it was Cliff's favorite season, and as he took a deep breath, the scent of summer's end filled his lungs.

The inhale did little to shake off his nerves. He had felt flustered since he woke in the early hours of the morning. In the Army, Cliff was used to the wakeups before dawn broke through the horizon; that habit had stayed with him through the years, despite leaving his branch seven years ago. Or leaving as much as someone could, he still kept a military-grade computer at his apartment and helped when requested.

Off in the distance, the sun began to rise above the mountainous tree line. Since moving to Carson, North Carolina, Cliff couldn't seem to get enough of watching the sun climb above the mountains, filling the sky with orange and pink hues. There was a time Cliff wasn't sure that he would ever see the light of the morning again.

He shook his head to clear his mind and reached up to push back the locks of dark hair that fell over his forehead. The cabin in the distance, just barely noticeable over the wheat field, glistened beneath the shadows as the sun's rays beamed down on the wooden structure.

The sound of rustling jerked Cliff's attention toward the bushes on his left. He watched as a gathering of does meandered through the field and headed toward the raspberry bushes near the cabin.

Just as he had hoped.

Perched on his knees, Cliff adjusted his scope and made sure that his target was centered in the frame.

After a few twists, he had a shot lined up exactly the way he wanted.

Perfect.

It only took him a moment to line up the scope, years of practice relied on his muscle memory. The deer don't even realize that he had his eyes set on them.

He filled his lungs, then held his breath as his finger hovered in the air. And with a soft exhale, Cliff let the sound of the click and shutter fill his mind.

Cliff pulled the camera away and glanced down at the small LCD screen. A smile grew on his lips as he inspected the final product.

Photography became his savior when he left the Army, it gave him something beautiful to focus on instead of the ugliness he had experienced for years.

As he stood from his knelt position in the field, Cliff tucked the camera back into his bag just as a swath of dark brown hair came into his line of sight. The ponytail swung with each step as its owner traveled down the dirt path by the cabin – his cabin. Or so he hoped one day. Maybe he missed his chance and this was the new owner.

Cliff was mesmerized by the person as she came closer to where he stood, utterly stagnant in the middle of the field. He watched as the woman turned the corner and that's when he got his first full glimpse of the most beautiful creature he'd ever laid eyes on.

A bright pink sports bra covered her strong and fit body, it barely contained her large breasts. Her lower half was wrapped in a pair of shorts no bigger than a bikini bottom.

He had been in Carson for three years and knew most of the residents, but this creature, this woman, wasn't someone that he recognized.

Nor did he acknowledge the ache in his chest as she passed in front of him, not even noticing his presence as she continued her quickened pace.

Cliff knew he needed to move from his spot, but he was frozen in place. He hadn't felt this visceral reaction to a woman since he was sixteen, and that thought scared the crap out of him.

Like pulling himself out of quicksand, Cliff lifted the concrete weight of his feet and took steps closer and closer to the dirt road until he found himself standing in the middle of the path. His focus was once again drawn to the back-and-forth swoosh of her hair as it swayed with her pace. His heartbeat quickened until it matched the same beat as her ponytail.

Who was this woman and why did she have this effect on me?

Since moving to Carson, Cliff had stayed away from women. The hurt from his past boiled near the surface anytime a woman had come on to him. But this one, with her bright colors and dark hair, had him wishing for something he hadn't wanted in years.

And that thought terrified him. Cliff had seen too much – knew too much. And though he was an asset in his prior career, and still was to some extent, it was not a lifestyle for everyone. He learned that one the hard way.

So why did this woman in her quick passing bring forth a vision of a future that will never exist?

A deep breath soothed him and Cliff turned on his heels as the woman ran out of his line of sight. The run-down cabin off in the distance took his attention once more. With his camera still in hand, he lifted the device to his eye and snapped a picture of the lone structure that barely stood on its foundation in the middle of the woods. To the naked eye, it would appear that a stiff wind could knock down the building, but Cliff knew better. He and that cabin were kindred spirits. To everyone else, they seemed to be rough and broken, but what they didn't witness was the strength in their bones. A solid force ensuring stability.

And like the sun that took her momentary spotlight off the cabin's roof, wielding her rays across the valley, Cliff knew that the mystery runner was his one ray of sunshine in the chaotic world of shadows that he lived in. He had felt awakened for the first time in years.

Heading toward his truck, Cliff cleared his mind of the woman that left him rattled. He had better things to do than to fantasize about a non-existent future. Instead, he steered his thoughts toward the tattoo shop he needed to open early for a client and a pit stop that needed to be had at his favorite diner to grab a quick breakfast.

But even as Cliff drove the needle into the soft skin of his friend's arm a few hours later, he couldn't rid his mind of the woman.

Cliff knew one thing for sure – he was in serious trouble.

Chapter One

"Hey, man. Good to see you," Cliff greeted his friend Harlan as he entered the tattoo shop. They clasped hands and went in for one of those one-armed man hugs.

Harlan and his band Exoneration had been on tour for the last few months, despite his wife's protests. But the band had taken a year and a half hiatus, and the short tour was required by their record label. Harlan's wife Cassidy and their two-year-old son, Ryan, threw him a party because they were so excited to have him home.

"Glad to be home," Harlan sighed, the relief evident in his words as he settled in the chair across from Cliff's station.

Harlan had called him last night during a bit of insomnia, asking if Cliff could fit him in today. There was no way he was going to turn down his friend because he knew what they would be working on. It was one of Cliff's favorite pieces to date.

When Harlan had married Cassidy, he wanted something unique to symbolize his love for his wife despite the days that they would spend apart with both of their demanding jobs. After a few minutes of discussion, Cliff had designed a dogwood tree in a way that he could continue to add leaves, branches, and flowers. A dogwood symbolized rebirth, an emotion Harlan felt whenever he returned home to his family. For every day that his friend was absent, they would add leaves to the tree to show his wife that she was always on his mind while he was gone.

Despite its beauty, Cliff knew that Harlan hated how many leaves were on the tree. There were also only three flowers – each representing a member of their family. It was no secret that Harlan and Cassidy wanted to increase that number.

Cliff hoped for his friend's sake that the number increased soon.

"So, anything new?" Cliff asked as he set up the ink and prepared to freehand the ninety-three leaves for the tree. At this point, the tree was going to meet completely around Harlan's waist soon,

"Naw, just happy to be home. I was so fired up to see Cassidy when I walked in the door that I almost locked her in the bedroom for the next few days. Too bad Ryan had other ideas. Who knew a two-year-old could be a cock block?" Harlan chuckled at his joke and Cliff couldn't help but join in. Harlan's brother-in-law, Logan, had the same complaint when he stopped by for a small tattoo last week. Except Logan had a trio of cock blockers with his three-year-old twins and a one-year-old.

"I'm sure you could ask Mrs. Connelly to watch Ryan for a few days so that you and Cassidy can have some alone time."

It was no secret that Amy Connelly adored her grandchildren and constantly requested more additions to the brood. Cliff almost felt like an adopted son to her with the way she stopped by and brought him dinner leftovers. She apparently had a notion in her head that he couldn't take care of himself. She knew little about his time on the battlefield, not only fending off the enemy, but fighting to stay alive with a lack of water and food.

With a subtle shake of his head, Cliff cleared his thoughts and went to work on finishing Harlan's piece. It only took about twenty minutes of Cliff expertly placing each leaf on the branches, looking as if they'd been there all along.

"You're all set."

"Thanks, man. What do I owe you?" Harlan asked as he reached for his wallet, but Cliff shook his head as he held up his hand. "No way, I'm not charging you."

"Dude, let me pay you."

"No, I don't want your money." Even with his recent purchase, Cliff didn't need Harlan's money, or anyone to pay for that matter. The shop did well enough with the tourists in the summer and fall seasons, and his checks from the military were sitting pretty in his savings account. He barely touched any of the funds. When his parents died in a car accident when Cliff was fifteen, they had left him a hefty life insurance payout that would take care of him for longer than he would ever live.

"Well, can I at least take you out to lunch?"

Cliff accepted his friend's request with a smile and cleaned up his space.

"The Grill or Angie's Diner?" Cliff asked as they stepped out of the shop, Cliff double-checked that the door locked behind him.

"I need to check in with Dylan if we can head toward The Grill," Harlan suggested. Dylan was the former FBI agent that ran The Grill, and the closest connection to the woman that left Cliff without a backward glance. He also happened to be married to Sydney, Cassidy's sister.

Cliff always liked Dylan and the two of them had worked on a few missions together when trouble found its way to their small town. He swore that Carson, North Carolina saw more action in two years than he had ever seen on the battlefield in that same amount of time.

The walk from the tattoo shop to The Grill, which shared space with Sydney's bakery, Wake and Bake, was short. It was just a block down Main Street which had seen a recent resurgence. The large department store that had gone out of business before Cliff had moved to town was now an indoor recreation center for the kids in town, which were growing in number at an astronomical rate; most of the Connelly family were the main contributors. There was now a brand-new retirement community about five miles away from the downtown center and so many wineries that Cliff had lost count. At the end of the main thoroughfare, the second bar in town was being cleaned out. It was a slow process done by a man that no one in town had seen except for a few quick glances. Cliff had tried to do some research on the man, but his searches came up empty. But, as long as he was here to better the community, Cliff saw no fault in the man keeping to himself. He heard from the Lady Busy Bees, the town gossipers, that the newcomer had applied for the proper licenses and permits to open a craft brewery. That information had Cliff thinking he had a new best friend in town.

Together, Harlan and Cliff walked through the door of The Grill, the bell chiming as they entered.

Sydney smiled warmly at them as they passed, her beauty took his breath away and Cliff turned his head quickly. Yeah, he may have had a little crush on the town's sweetheart when he moved to town. But he knew that she was happily married to Dylan – a guy that he liked and respected. Together they had helped save her from a kidnapping that kept Cliff up at night.

"Hey, Sparta," Cliff greeted Dylan with the nickname he bestowed on the man at their first meeting. He perched on one of the diner's barstools and Harlan did the same.

"This is an unexpected surprise. What kind of trouble am I in to have both of you two assholes in my place?" the man in the white apron said in jest.

Harlan spoke up first. "Nothing at all. Cassidy wanted me to ask you and Sydney if you all wanted to join us for dinner. Ryan has been asking to see Maddelyn and Alice." It wasn't a town secret that Sydney and Dylan struggled to have children. So, when they showed up at her brother Ryker's wedding reception with baby Maddelyn, the town was happily surprised. Little did anyone expect the second surprise that she was also pregnant at the time. Their youngest Alice was only seven months younger than Maddelyn.

"I don't think that will be a problem, but are you sure? We know you just got back from tour."

"Yeah, it was fine. Maybe it will tire Ryan out and he'll sleep through the night. Six sound okay?"

"Sure. What can I get you both to eat?"

Cliff and Harlan ordered their sandwiches and Cliff listened quietly as his friend and Dylan gossiped like a bunch of old ladies. He had always been more of an observer, probably what made him a great sniper and Army Ranger. He usually knew what someone was going to do before they did. Just as he knew that Sydney was going to walk over and give him a hug.

It only took two minutes before he felt her hand touch his exposed forearm and he turned to welcome her embrace.

"Cliff, I'm so glad that you're here. I have a question for you."

"Sure, what's up?"

"Well, you know that I love that picture you took of the lake. The one with the dock. Do you think I could get something again like that, but a panoramic shot with the dock in the center? I want to do a few canvases in our bedroom, so when we wake up in the morning, we're waking up to a lake view."

Cliff remembered the shot. It was one he took the day before Alexis had barged into his life. The woman with the swaying ponytail that haunted his every thought for years.

"Sure, I can do that."

It wouldn't be hard; the lake was on his property. One of the few large purchases he made.

"You're the best. Thank you," she exclaimed as she lifted up on her toes and kissed his cheek. He could feel his skin heat beneath her lips and Cliff tried to duck his head in embarrassment.

Like a whirlwind, Sydney spun on her heels and swooshed through the side door into Dylan's kitchen.

Cliff and Harlan watched the love-sick man move behind his own door, disappearing to see his wife.

Cliff continued to eat his sandwich in silence, mentally going through the list of clients he had for the day and the inventory he needed to order to get ready for their busy season. Spring was coming to a close and summer was rearing her head earlier than usual.

Taking a final bite of his lunch, Cliff smacked Harlan on the shoulder and thanked him for the impromptu lunch before heading back toward his shop. But he didn't step through the front door. Instead, he went around the back and climbed the stairs that led to the apartment he once occupied above his shop.

This was the secret domain that only a select few knew about. Sure, many suspected that it was his apartment, but it was so much more than that. Until recently, he had been a part of an underground government agency working to gather information on a drug cartel that was dabbling in sex trafficking. Unfortunately, that mission had recently been shut down and Cliff had been waiting anxiously for a new assignment. Though drawing and photography eased his mind, let him see the beauty in the world, his covert missions gave him a sense of purpose.

Stepping into the main room, Cliff booted up the computer that looked like it was straight out of 1998 and typed in a name. Alexis Alta. The woman he couldn't get out of his mind and a woman with almost as much government clearance as himself.

Seven hundred and sixty-two days since he saw her last, but she wasn't far from his mind. A silhouetted version of her constantly played in his daydreams.

The computer pinged when it came up empty. The same sound it'd made for the last year whenever he searched for her. Cliff didn't know why the compulsion to make sure she was safe possessed him, but he knew that it was impossible to turn off. He had tried, tried so damn hard to forget her. Forget her smile, forget the small tinkle in her laugh, forget the haunting brown eyes that held more secrets than they could handle. She was his undoing and she didn't even know it.

Sighing as he shut down his computer, Cliff leaned back in the chair, his hands rested on top of his overgrown hair.

He hated this feeling of being weak. This feeling as though someone needed his help, but he's powerless to do anything. Alexis was smart, Cliff knew she was more than capable of taking care of herself, but the last check-in he was able to find had her along the Mexican border infiltrating a drug cartel.

Cliff didn't let anyone knew he was keeping an eye on Alexis because he knew his friends would bend over backward to try to get him the same happiness that they were all experiencing. He had his chance at a happily-ever-after, but his career burned that hope into a pile of ash on the ground. Cliff and his bride barely said "I do" before their world changed forever.

An alarm sounded across the hall, and he almost fell from his chair as he startled. His first appointment would be arriving in five minutes and he needed to unlock the front door.

Taking two steps at a time, Cliff used the interior stairs taking him to the storage area of his shop.

On the way to the front door, he took a glance at the calendar, remembering that his part-time receptionist would start next week along with a second tattoo artist. Their background checks came back clean and neither had any outstanding red flags on the other tests he liked to run.

Cliff used to be able to run the shop by himself, but the last two summer and fall seasons had him turning people away. Not something Cliff wanted to repeat this year. He felt lucky to find two people wanting to move to the small town of Carson. Though he made sure to warn them that once you step inside the town, they may find it hard to leave.

Moving to the door, he flipped the lock and turned on the neon sign signifying that the shop was open.

Back at his booth, Cliff set up the ink and gun he'd need for the appointment then grabbed his camera out of the bag that sat in the corner of his booth. He hadn't taken many pictures recently, his time spread thin between the shop and renovating his new house. Cliff felt a pang in his chest as the weight of the camera settled in his hand. Photography had a way of relaxing him, making him feel as if he was one with whatever it was he was capturing on display.

Flipping the small LCD screen toward him, he pressed the button that allowed him to scroll through the images. Just as it landed on a picture of a woman's back, the chime above his door sounded, alerting him to his customer.

Stepping out of the booth, he marched toward the small waiting area and greeted the older man.

"Good afternoon, what can I do for you today?" Cliff asked as he shook the man's hand.

Together they moved toward the booth as Cliff listened to the man describe the dragon he wanted along his forearm. Immediately he sought out his portfolio for a design he had drawn last week, and the man only asked for a small change.

It didn't take Cliff long to print it on the transfer paper and line it up how the man wanted. The motions were automatic as he drew the ink onto the needle and swiped it slowly across the man's skin, wiping every so often with a paper towel to see the progression.

He got lost in the movement, in the flow, as he permanently etched the design on the man. Normally it would have been enough to keep his focus far away from Alexis and her whereabouts, but he had a sinking suspicion that even the mundaneness of his day wasn't going to keep his desires at bay.

No matter how hard he wished them away.

***

Her breath was steady as she crept along the side of the deserted building. Except, she and her team knew what was lurking beneath the floorboards. Alexis and her team had been working for over a year to infiltrate and gather enough evidence to take down this drug ring.

That was all the mission called for at first, but their recent intel discovered the groundwork for an undercover sex ring.

There was not a single thing that fired Alexis up more than sex trafficking. When she heard the news, she had been ready to rush the entire process with guns blazing. She was so keyed up that her boss required her to take two weeks of personal leave to get her head on straight. Alexis didn't understand at the time. She didn't understand how the men on her team could sit back and continue to let this happen, even though she knew they didn't have enough evidence. All she could see in that angered haze of red were people's wives, sisters, mothers drugged and carried off to who-knew-where.

"What's your position?" a voice asked in her ear. The small device sat snugly in her ear canal that Alexis almost forgot that she was wearing it.

"We're on the south side of the building. Was the picture coming in clear?" she asked Heath of the small camera attached to her bulletproof vest.

Alexis and Heath had been assigned to the same missions since they were both recruited by the FBI. He was the closest thing she had to a brother and she loved him fiercely. She knew, without a doubt, that he would have her back, just as she would have his.

And tonight, she needed his eyes and ears. There was no moonlight guiding them, just a few night-vision goggles and the keen eye of Heath through the camera. The team she was working with were talented, but it was the first time the eight of them had been placed together. These kinds of missions were always difficult, but when you were working with new people, it was hard to gauge if they would have your back. And from Alexis' standpoint – they didn't.

Their director had explained the plan to them before they left the New Mexico office. Charlie and Ted were to enter the bunker first, followed by Alexis and the rest of the team. But when they arrived on the scene, Charlie (who had announced himself the mission's leader) rearranged the lineup.

Which was why Alexis now stood in front of the group, peering her head around the corner to make sure it was clear before they breached the Eastern entrance.

"All clear," the crackling voice of Heath sounds in her ear.

With a flick of her wrist, Alexis motioned for the men to move around her and stand guard as she pressed her body against the wall slipping inside the door. She held her breath, listening for any movements as she raised her gun at eye level, poised and trained to take anything out that so much as took a step in her direction.

But as expected, the room was empty.

She and the team moved quickly toward the basement entrance. She had hoped that they could have found the outlet on the other side of the Mexican border to trap the cartel in place, but cooperation with multiple teams was futile.

Primed at the base of the stairs, Alexis leaned down slightly to check for clearance and found a barren hallway. The team followed her down the steps and through the narrow passageway. The walls were shrinking around them until they could only pass through in a single line.

"Something's not right," Alexis whispered, knowing Heath was monitoring a surveillance drone they had hovering over the property.

"Then get out of there," he replied.

She immediately imagined the scared looks on the women and children that had been taken by these drug lords and Alexis knew that there was no turning back for her, she'd see this through to the end.

"I couldn't. We couldn't. There was literally no place to go. Check the tracking against the layout. How much farther do we have?"

They had been lucky that their intel was able to provide a layout of the underground bunker, and the man knew the consequences if he tried to pull one over on their team.

"Five yards ahead, you'll find an entrance on the left."

"Charlie," Alexis whispered, "run an infrared scan."

The group paused and Charlie stepped around Alexis, leaning the infrared camera into the opening, scanning the space for any heat. As he gave the all-clear, Alexis motioned for the team to follow her inside the room.

The darkness swelled around them, threatening to suffocate them in the abandoned room. Alexis' heart pounded in her chest, sounding like she was running a marathon. Her fear spiked and the earlier notion of something being wrong bubbled to the surface.

This room should have had men gathered or standing watch. The team knew how this cartel worked and they always covered their backs.

Alexis paused, the group halting behind her, and she glanced around the room with her night-vision goggles. Nothing seemed out of place, just a room with a few chairs and a table. A dark stain marred the corner and Alexis shivered at the thought of what may have occurred there.

"Let's move forward," Charlie barked, stepping around Alexis and waving his hand toward the group.

Ted immediately moved to follow his friend farther into the room, but the rest of the men stood stoically behind Alexis. She knew that they're waiting for her decision to proceed.

But something nagged at her – something wasn't right.

Just as Alexis began to call out for the team to fall back, Charlie and Ted stepped farther into the room toward another exit. She held in a deep inhale as they opened the door and moved into another hallway.

The rest of the group followed the two men down the hallway, leaving Alexis at the rear. She kept her eyes peeled, twisting and turning her head, continually taking in their surroundings.

She remembered the layout from the map and knew the hall led to six more rooms with the possibility of no outlet, at least not one that their intel could recollect.

They traveled farther down the narrow path, passing two doors that Charlie claimed to show no heat signature. Her feet faltered when the thud of a door shutting sounded behind her.

"Stop," she called out in a breathy shout, but the men didn't hear.

Alexis turned behind her and aimed her gun as she scanned the space. Though they've traveled quite a distance, she could see the door that led to this second hallway was now closed.

Her heart falters at the notion that they're not alone.

"Fallback, team. Fallback!" Alexis shouted to the group only to have Charlie overrule her. "Continue forward!"

His yell was muffled by the first round of shots. Alexis looked around in horror as two of her men fell onto the concrete floor, both taking shots to the head and neck.

"Shots fired!" Alexis screeched.

"Get the fuck out of there, Alexis!" Heath roars in her ear.

"Couldn't trapped. Find me a way out." Reaching out, Alexis held her hand against the neck of one of the downed men, trying to stop the blood flow and hating that his pulse was weakening.

She knew that if anyone could save her and the members of her team, it was Heath.

Closing her eyes, Alexis leaned away from the dying man and pressed her back against the wall tucking herself into a ball toward the ground. She wasn't cowering – far from it. In the group home as a teenager, Alexis learned how to intensify her hearing. She could close her eyes and listen for every ping and crackle to know when someone was approaching, which was always helpful when one of the older boys would try to enter the girl's rooms.

Her previous teams and friends liked to call her a ninja. She was quick, stealthy, and despite her small stature, she was powerful.

Alexis closed off from the world around her and listened. She could hear her own heartbeat, hear her shallow breaths with each inhale, hear the screams of her men as they tried to outrun the bullets in the blackened hallway.

Whoosh, whoosh.

The hiss of bullets passing by her ears had her fighting the urge to jump in response. They came from her left side – the side facing her men. She listened again. The sound of bullets cracking against the concrete mixed seamlessly with the cries of her team.

Whoosh, whoosh, whoosh.

Three more shots. All from the same direction. From her estimate, they were coming down at an angle, possibly from the ceiling. With her goggles in place, Alexis held her gun in the direction she heard the shot and fired blindly. She emptied the magazine and reloaded as more bullets buzzed across her ear. One coming too eerily close to her cheek that she felt the kiss of air.

Steadying her breath, Alexis stood from her perch on the floor, her back pressed against the cold concrete threatening to seep into her skin, her heavy clothes doing little to provide warmth.

With a quick glance at the floor with the night-vision goggles, she took in the massacre before her. The men's screams had stopped, their shallow breaths fading into the background of the bullets still echoing in the hall.

"I found an exit. Go back to the room on your right. There was a false air vent that leads to a ground-level door. You'll have to find a way to get up there, but that's your only way out. The rest of the cartel was entering the bunker as we speak."

Swallowing against the lump in her throat, Alexis said, "I couldn't leave my men."

It was a creed she'd always followed, so had Heath. So, it surprised her as he said, "If you want to live, you have to. They're almost gone, Alex. I'm not getting a reading on any of them. Now get out of there."

She took one final glance at the men that had worked beside her for the last few weeks and whispered a prayer that she remembered.

Resolute, Alexis cleared her mind of the ambush and slinked her way back toward the room she had walked past, constantly scanning her surroundings with her gun drawn. The handle of the door pressed into her hip, and without turning around, Alexis twisted the knob from behind and slipped into the room, praying that she wouldn't find anyone inside.

Slowly she closed the door, her hand still holding the twisted knob to avoid as little sound as possible. Alexis turned on her heels, scanned the room with her gun, and breathed a sigh of relief to find it empty.

"The room was all clear," she relayed to Heath.

Through the earpiece, she could hear a struggle. Alexis paused, not knowing if her friend was being attacked or killed while she's stuck in this room, helpless.

"Heath! Heath, what's going on?"

"Sorry, Alex. Had some douche try to sneak up on me. Don't you worry, I got him taken care of. Now, let's get you out of there."

The relief that washed over her was immediate and overwhelming. She didn't want this mission to go more awry than it already was.

Knowing that her friend was safe, Alexis frantically searched for a way to reach the vent, but the room was empty. Nothing except her and the cold concrete – and her lack of height.

"I couldn't get out this way. I have no way to reach the vent."

Shit. She knew where there were chairs though, but backtracking seemed like her worst possible nightmare. And she knew by now that the upper level of the bunker was going to be swarmed with cartel members.

"Heath, I have to go back to the basement entrance. I can get a chair from that room. It was my only way out."

Alexis heard his muffled curses before he agreed to her plan, promising to keep watch through the drone and her on-person camera.

As she exited from the room back into the hallway, she was greeted by silence. The shooting had stopped, but she didn't doubt for a second that she was in the clear. Using soft, swift steps, Alexis strode back to the end of the hallway. The opening that she had left opened, now closed as she had heard not five minutes before. She should have turned back at that point, saved the team. But hindsight was an unyielding demon. It would devour you from the inside, leaving you rotting in regret.

The first thing she noticed as she slowly opened the door was that light illuminated the space. The once haunting square of concrete now resembled a mildewed storage room.

Voices sounded in the distance, far enough away that she should be able to grab the chair and leave without notice.

But as she stepped into the space Alexis realized that she should have known better. This entire mission was a catastrophe from the start. Why would this moment turn out differently?

The instant her hand touched the back of the chair, the series of voices traveled down from the steps. They approached the room and Alexis knew that her time was limited.

Thinking on her feet, she grabbed a second chair and lifted them both under her arms as she performed an about-face into the hallway. Alexis placed one of the chairs on the floor and maneuvered the other in front of her body, preparing to lodge it under the doorknob to buy her some time. It wouldn't be a lot, but she'd take any few extra seconds that she could.

The men filed into the room with a woman tied up and dragging behind them. Alexis could see that the fight in her was gone and she had succumbed to the death sentence she was about to endure.

Alexis' body flinched at the sight, and she knew if she didn't escape that she'd be in the same position as the woman. Her need to fight took over her body.

Hastily she reached for the knob of the door, preparing to close it before anyone witnessed her presence, their focus on their prisoner in the corner. But as a final man entered, Alexis couldn't hold back the gasp that escaped her lips.

He's dressed to the nines. Full three-piece black suit, pocket square and matching tie, shoes shinier than slick ice. He's a man of power and fear with a face that Alexis could never forget. How could she when she wore a constant reminder of him around her neck?

Whether he could sense her company or merely heard her gasp of air, she'd never knew. But Alexis made no mistake that his eyes mirrored the same amount of confusion as hers when they landed on her face just as she closed the door completely.

With a shove, she heaved the chair under the doorknob, locking the door in place temporarily. As if the god Mercury had taken over her body, Alexis moved as fast as lightning through the hall to the abandoned room.

With the help of the chair, she was able to remove the vent cover and jump into the metal shaft.

"Which way, Heath?"

"Go to your right five yards, then you'll meet a fake barrier."

She aimlessly followed his direction in the bleakness until her head bumped against a wall. With all her might, Alexis shoved at the false wall until it gave way. Dirt and rocks crumbled around her as she maneuvered her body out of the tunnel.

"I'm out," she breathed in relief as she pushed up from her knees to stand.

"Head two miles to your left toward the canal then continue for five miles. That's where I'll pick you up."

Alexis scrambled away from the opening, tripping over her own feet in the process, the sandy ground coating her hands as she braced herself against the fall. But she knew there was no time to waste, the sounds of heavy feet closed in as the goonies raced after her.

She weaved in and out of trees until she reached the small canal of water Heath described.

"I'm at the water," Alexis declared as she moved back into the tree line, staying out of the sight of the men chasing her. Thank goodness for the years in high school running long-distance because if there was ever a time to need the stamina to run for long distances, then that was this moment.

Steadying her breaths, Alexis listened to the pounding of her feet on the ground as she weaved around the trees and bushes. To her horror, an opening lay ahead, and knowing that she's only about three miles into her trek, she realized that she's about to make herself an open target.

The men couldn't be too far behind her, they don't appear to be the kind that gave up easily. With a deep inhale, letting the air fill her lungs, Alexis prepared herself for the sprint.

She turned to look over her shoulder and caught the eye of a man quickly approaching. She aimed her gun in his direction and pulled the trigger. Her shot hit the target dead-on, a surprise to Alexis due to her wavering energy, and the man fell to the ground.

Four more men approached her line of sight, just far enough away that she should be able to cut across the clearing just in time – hopefully.

With one final prayer, Alexis tucked her gun in its holster, took a deep breath, and ran for her life. Her feet pounded the surface, the dark night sky doing little to illuminate the area around her. She's thankful for the night-vision goggles that offered some form of illumination.

But the other men must have a pair as well because just as she reached the endpoint of her sprint, a bullet soared by her head, lodging itself in a nearby tree.

Three more shots fire off.

Pain. Excruciating pain overtook her as bullets hit her shoulder and thigh, both threatening to bring her to her knees. But Alexis knew that if she faltered now, she'd have no escape. This was her only chance out.

Miraculously she made it to the woods and ducked behind a large tree truck, hunkering down toward the ground, as close to the sandy soil as possible. Ripping her gun free from its holster, she peered around the tree, trigger poised at the ready.

Despite the wound on her dominant shoulder, she knew she could still expertly aim and shoot; Alexis always practiced shooting giving both hands time on the trigger.

The first man came within the scope and Alexis fired off two shots, then turned her attention to the other three men approaching, proficiently taking them out as well.

She continued to scan the surrounding area, not finding anything amiss, then turned back behind the tree.

"Heath, I've been hit. Took out five men. I'm just outside the clearing."

"Sit tight until I've located you. Don't move."

Her vision began to swirl as she rested against the tree. Through the haze Alexis slipped her belt free from her pants and fastened it around her thigh, just above the bullet wound. She tensed as she took in the amount of blood pouring from her leg and couldn't imagine that her shoulder looked any better.

"I'm losing a lot of blood."

"Fuck. I'm coming for you, okay? Don't go out on me," Heath cried out. "I'll be there in fifteen minutes."

Alexis did her best to stay coherent, but the need to close her eyes was overwhelming. Her body fell to the right, landing on her injured shoulder and leg, a grunt sounds from her throat at the contact.

She knew that her consciousness was slipping away. Too much blood loss. Too much adrenaline. Too much fear.

Slipping the goggles from her eyes, she peered up at the night sky through the trees, a lone star twinkling far off in the distance.

"Heath. When was the last time you stared up at the sky? I mean *really* looked at the stars?"

She knew that her words were on the edge of peculiarity, but couldn't find a way to restrain them.

"Alexis? Hang on. I'm close."

"Oh, the pretty star is fading. That's sad." Even to her own ears, she knew that she sounds different, spoke differently.

"If I die, will you. . ."

"You're not going to die, Alexis."

"I'm going to go to sleep now. So tired," she whispered, unsure if Heath could make out her voice.

She heard her name off in the distance, a gentle buzzing in her ear as she settled in to sleep. Behind her closed eyes, Alexis' mind lands on an image of a man with brown eyes before the shadows encompassed her completely.

Chapter Two

Angie's diner was one of Cliff's favorite places. Not only was it a hub for everyone in town, but it overflowed with local gossip. He could subtly learn whatever he needed without attracting attention to himself.

At one time, Cliff feared places like this one. The fear of everyone watching his next move, fear of someone with a more sinister plot following him through the diner's red door and hurting the people that welcomed him without question.

It took years, and a hearty push by the Lady Busy Bees, for him to willingly come inside the restaurant. Now it was so routine the servers knew what to bring him based on which day of the week it was. Predictability was one of Cliff's mottos.

Years spent overseas, days and nights moving him to thousands of different locations, took its toll. Cliff gave up on the idea of spontaneity a long time ago.

"Same as usual, sugar?" Ethel, the older waitress, asked with a wink.

"You got it," he replied as he moved toward the back of the diner, sliding onto the vinyl bench with his gaze trained on the door. He may not be active duty any longer, but knowing who was coming and going gave him a sense of peace. The large room in the back, used for banquets and parties, was only open at dinner or special occasions, so he knew there would be no surprises.

"Here's your coffee. I'll have your food right out." Ethel sat the steaming mug in front of him and scurried back behind the counter.

Cliff sipped from the mug, watching the older crowd disperse from their stools as younger couples and families descended on the restaurant. It was Saturday, and in Carson, that meant the Farmer's Market was about to be in full swing. It took Cliff a while to feel comfortable in the oversized crowd. Not only the locals attended the two-block gathering, but vendors and residents from six counties surrounding Carson came in full force. Especially when the weather was as nice as it was on this particular weekend.

A few minutes later, Ethel sat down a plate with Cliff's breakfast. The smell of the perfectly cooked bacon and scrambled eggs reached his nose. A sudden memory popped into his mind of the last time he had scrambled eggs before moving to Carson and his heart clenched.

"Can I get you anything else?"

Shaking his mind free of the memory, Cliff turned his attention toward Ethel and smiled. "This looks delicious. Thank you."

With an over-exaggerated motion, Ethel flicked her hand up and down in front of her face as if cooling herself off. "Whew. Son, if you keep smiling like that, the brains of every woman in town will be scrambled like those eggs."

The older woman walked away continuing to fan herself, leaving Cliff to his meal. But just as he lifted a hearty forkful of the egg to his mouth the bench across from him squeaked. Without lifting his head, Cliff looked across the table to find his friend Logan, a local doctor and Avery Connelly's husband, looking at him with narrowed eyes. The man gave off an air of anger and Cliff wasn't quite sure why.

"Hey, man." Cliff greeted his friend, trying to defuse the situation as he took a bite of food on the fork still held in the air.

"You missed Mama Connelly's dinner last Sunday."

It was a well-established rule in Carson that if you were invited to the Connelly's family dinner on Sundays, you were expected to attend. But Cliff had been asked every week for the last two years and declined every single time.

"I've never made it to a single one. I'm surprised she still asked."

A look of disbelief and shock registered on Logan's face and Cliff had to wonder if there was something he was missing.

"You helped save and protect her family, Cliff. She considers you family."

"Which means. . .?" Cliff let the question hang in the air for a moment.

"Which means you need to be there."

Eyeing his friend, Cliff set down his fork and leaned against the back of the booth.

"No catch?" His friend started to shake his head, but Cliff added, "And don't forget I can take out a man without lifting a finger, literally."

He watched as Logan's Adam's apple pulsed up and down his neck as he swallowed.

"Fine. She may be trying to set you up with some of the local girls. She's found a new hobby in matchmaking."

Lifting another forkful of food to his lips, Cliff pointed out, "I don't need help finding a woman."

Logan gazed at him skeptically, but it was the truth. Cliff could go home with a willing woman if he ever took them up on their advances.

Cliff's attention was drawn back to Logan as his friend slipped from the booth, leaning on the edge of the table with his fists balled up on the chipped Formica. "When was the last time you went on an actual date? When was the last time that you did anything for yourself?"

Cliff tried to think back. The last time he went on a date was. . .the day before he was shipped out at eighteen, leaving a grieving bride at home. Had it really been that long? By the blank look on Cliff's face, Logan must have gotten his answer.

"Exactly. Don't dismiss Mrs. Connelly next time she asks. Plus, it may not be me that gets the pleasure of convincing you next time."

The Connelly family was a big one with six children, three of whom were brothers. Add in the husbands of the sisters and you have one gigantic clan of men he liked to consider friends. But he knew the family would always come first, and if that meant knocking some sense into Cliff until he understood his position as an adopted Connelly, then he wouldn't put it past them. They'd do anything to please their parents.

"Fine, I'll make sure to reconsider the invite next time. Now, can I get back to eating my breakfast before it gets cold?" Cliff asked trying to feign annoyance, but he knew that he was failing. His friend's face morphed into a delighted grin.

"See that you do. Avery, the kids, and I are here for a quick bite before going to the market. I know she would be thrilled if you joined us today."

"Sure, I had plans to stop by the shop this morning if you guys don't mind."

"Yeah?" Logan asked, a glint of excitement flashed across the man's face. "I had a few thoughts for some additions on the new tattoo you gave me. Maybe we can talk about it while we're there." He turned his head as the bell over the diner door chimed and Logan watched his family stroll into the diner and settle at a booth near the front. Their twins scurried across the bench seat on their knees, while their toddler sat on Avery's lap.

Cliff envied his friend, both he and Avery deserved every ounce of happiness that had come their way. And if his instincts were correct, then Cliff foresaw another addition to their brood in another seven months or so.

"Just grab me when you're ready to go. I'll work my way through the paper while I wait."

Nodding, Logan left with a glazed look of happiness on his face, seemingly as much in love today as he was when he first met his wife. It seemed that all of his friends got that same starry-eyed look on their faces when they saw their spouse or significant other. When he had been married, Cliff couldn't remember ever wearing that expression when he saw his wife.

Shoulders nudged and brushed against Cliff as he traveled down the street of the market. As predicted, the idyllic weather had brought people from all over. Vendor tents and canopies lined the entire six blocks of Main Street, about four blocks more than average. The spectrum of colors cast the thoroughfare in a prism of colors.

A woman tugging a wagon filled to the brim with frames and canvases pushed passed their group, jostling Avery in the process. On instinct, Cliff reached out and wrapped an arm around Avery's slender shoulders to help steady her on her feet. Logan stood on his other side pushing their oversized stroller through the crowd, his face fuming at the woman's retreating back.

"You okay?" Cliff asked the petite woman as she brushed her hand across the arm that the stranger knocked into.

"Yeah," she began, but as she stared up at Cliff something in his gaze must have registered with her. "You know, don't you? Logan, did you tell him?"

Logan shouted back at her, "Tell him what?"

"Ugh, you're like the freaking baby whisperer. We haven't even told my family yet." Cliff knew that Avery was trying her hardest to sound upset that he spoiled her secret, but her utter happiness quickly extinguished any forceful anger.

"I won't tell anyone. You know that your secret was safe with me."

Her blue eyes danced in elation as the corner of her lips tilted upward in a smile. "You're like a vault. But someday, a woman is going to break that code. Mark my word."

"I'm shaking in my boots," he replied in mock fear.

"Are you patronizing me? This morning is getting weirder and weirder. First, the kids let me sleep in, now you're being sarcastic and laughing, I don't know what to expect next."

With false hurt, Cliff holds a hand to his chest as he said, "I joke."

"No, you don't," Logan chimed in as he steered the stroller toward the booth where Sydney and Dylan had set up in front of her bakery selling coffee and her legendary donuts.

As they reached the booth, Cliff waved off and continued toward his shop another block down the way. Logan and Dylan followed in line, leaving the women at the stand.

The bustling crowd of people seemed to part like the Red Sea as the trio made their way on the path. As they approached the shop, Cliff took in the vendor parked in front of his store. Shirley and Temple Fitzgerald sat in their chairs pretending to sell flowers as they sip on glasses of lemonade. And if Cliff were a betting man, he would put his life savings on those two women having a little something extra mixed in with their beverage.

Snagging his keys from his pockets, Cliff unlocked the door and gestured for his friends to enter the shop before turning the deadbolt to lock it again. One time he came into the shop during the Farmer's

RENEE HARLESS

Market and a group of college-aged assholes swarmed his place. It was not a scenario he wanted to repeat, especially since they were rowdy and didn't end up getting any ink. They were mainly there for the cool air.

"What kind of art were you thinking?" Cliff asked Logan as he stepped behind the front desk and took a peek at his calendar. He had a few appointments today, but the remainder of his week was pretty clear as his shift worker was set to start.

"I was thinking of getting a chest piece. I love the phoenix on my back and the thumb prints you just did for the kids, but I want to get something that represents Avery, you know?"

Nodding, Cliff pulled put a few designs he has been working on and showed them to his friend. They talked about different elements that Logan liked from each piece and together they decided to put them all together.

After they set up Logan's appointment for later in the week, Cliff turned to Dylan, and the man sheepishly told him that he was there to invite Cliff to the Connelly dinner the next evening.

"Dude, please. Sydney was threatening to deny me."

"Deny you what?" Cliff asked, enjoying watching his friend squirm in the hot seat. If Cliff was going to endure being set up at a family dinner, then his friend could stew for a few minutes.

"She has my cock and balls on a leash man. Do this for me and I'll get any intel that I can on Alexis."

That immediately had Cliff straightening his spine. Only a select few knew about his curiosity toward the raven-haired beauty.

"How do you. . .?" Cliff let the question hang in the air. His breath came in shallow pants as the terror that one of his secrets had come to light.

"You're not the only one that still has a government job on the down-low. And we all saw the way you looked at her."

Cliff hadn't been given a chance to meet Alexis like the rest of the Connelly's. He was rewarded with a meeting and a handshake as Dylan gave a low down on how they had planned to find Sydney when she was kidnapped. When their hands touched, Cliff felt like he had known her already, knew all of her deepest desires and secrets. It wasn't just an operative meeting for him and he had wanted nothing more than to steal her away, strip her bare, and make her his.

But Alexis had pulled her hand away and stayed focused on the mission at hand. To anyone else, she appeared like the consummate professional that she was. But he had seen the dilation of her eyes when their palms brushed. And when she had tripped over her own feet as they exited the meeting behind Dylan, he was the one that felt her grip on his arm last a beat too long.

She had buried herself under his skin.

Trying to brush off his friend's declaration, Cliff began to pull out items he'd need for his first appointment. "Not sure how since I can count on one hand how many times I've been in the same room as her."

"Doesn't mean we didn't see the look," Logan chimed in.

Curious, Cliff made the mistake of asking, "What look?"

"You know the one. Where your eyes get big and a dopey grin settles on your face. Don't worry, we've all had it," Dylan explains.

"Hell, I still have it," Logan added, perfectly executing the expression in question as if he were thinking of his wife.

"You both are full of shit."

"You keep telling yourself that." Dylan stepped closer and leaned toward him. A few inches separated their face. "But, I'm the one that knows how many times you've pinged her name in the last two years on the computer in your not-so-secret lair upstairs."

As his friend returned to his full height, Cliff wondered what else Dylan knew about him and considered cornering his friend to learn the details, but decided against it.

The prospect of learning more, or anything, about Alexis was too high. She'd had this magnetic pull on him since they first met over three years ago and the force was just as strong today as it was then – for him anyway. She was one of the only people he couldn't get a good read on.

"Fine, I'll be there tomorrow. Do *not* let Mrs. Connelly try to set me up, or I'll leave."

"No, you won't. But I'll pass that note along anyway. My dick thanks you."

Adding fuel to the flame, Cliff added, "Tell Sydney I said hello," knowing that it would rile Dylan up. And sure enough, the man clenched his fists at his sides.

"Fucker," the man mumbled under his breath as he turned to exit the shop, Logan followed suit.

"See ya tomorrow," Cliff called out with a laugh as he watched the man leave the shop. He headed to the front door to lock it back in place before returning to his station.

For the first time in a few weeks, Cliff had the urge to go out in the field and capture nature's beauty with his camera. He sat back in his chair and wondered if the notion of family had something to do with that or if it was the mention of the woman that he couldn't get out of his mind.

Family. It has to be family.

Cliff knocked on the front door of the Connelly's home. The red door opened wide before his knuckles left the wooden surface and Amy tugged him into her arms. Despite her petite stature, Amy gripped him tightly within her embrace, his breath leaving his lungs in a whoosh.

"Cliff, I am so glad you could make it."

Feeling admonished at his actions, Cliff sheepishly replied, "I figured it was time to make an appearance. Thank you for having me, Mrs. Connelly."

"Amy, please." She stepped around him and closed the front door before leading him through her house toward the ample dining space. Cliff had been in the house before, but always under the worst reasons. The Connelly's were a target for bad luck and usually required Cliff's sniper and reconnaissance expertise, not that he ever minded. With a family of billionaires, rock stars, and celebrities, it was almost inevitable that bad shit would find them. Luckily, it had been quiet on their home front since all of the children were married off. Fate had a strange way of bringing people together.

But tonight, Cliff was here on good terms, better terms. The table was filled to the brim with food and every available seat at the extended table was occupied. Every seat except the one next to Amy. As he passed by his friends, all the men smiled knowingly while the women nudged their husbands, silently thanking them for getting Cliff to accept the invitation.

He breathed a sigh of relief when he noticed no random woman awaiting his arrival either.

"This looks delicious, Amy. Good to see you, Mr. Connelly." Cliff made sure to shake the hand of the man that raised his best friends. It was a surprise to even see him at dinner considering he was the fire chief in the town, providing both fire and rescue assistance in the town as needed. The town's budget only allowed for one hired employee, volunteers provided the rest of the help. Even Cliff made it a point to aid when he could, but with the influx of residents to the town and the new retirement community opening in a few weeks, he knew that Joseph was stretched thin. Cliff, along with hundreds of others in a town hall meeting, have petitioned the mayor to increase the fire and rescue budget.

Cliff sat silently as he ate his meal, humbly listening to the conversations flowing around him. Despite the siblings bickering back and forth, he could hear that their words were filled with love. Growing up, Cliff had always dreamed of having a family as large as this one. But it wasn't in the cards for him then and it wasn't in the deck now.

As the dinner ended, Amy stepped away and returned with a few pies as dessert. Saliva pooled in his mouth at the thought of devouring a slice of Amy's famous apple pie.

The matriarch plates him a large slice and he holds the scalloped edged plate with reverence. Taking a hearty bite, the crusty edges with the sweet inside melted in Cliff's mouth and he has to fight back a groan of appreciation.

"This is the best pie I've ever had, Amy."

"Why thank you, Cliff. It is nice to see someone taking the time to enjoy it instead of scarfing it down like everyone else at the table," the mother of the family admonished. The table grew so quiet that the ticking of the clock on the fireplace mantle could be heard.

Cliff chuckled, his laughter breaking through the silence of the room and quickly others began to join in. The group offered their apologies to Amy before diving back into their desserts, but he didn't miss the wink she aimed in his direction before enjoying her own piece of pie.

Down at the other end of the table, Dylan stood abruptly with his phone pressed to his ear, Sydney watched with alarm. Her expressive brown eyes bulged with alarm and her hand pressed to her mouth. Something has happened and by their expressions, Cliff was guessing that the news wasn't a good one.

The people in the room stared and listened as Dylan gave one-word answers to the caller on the phone, his face developing an ashen shade with each passing moment. Cliff's fear spiked, his skin grew clammy in expectancy as Dylan met his gaze. Patience had never been Cliff's strong suit, and the seconds that passed were agonizing. Like shards of thin paper, Cliff's skin felt as if it was being torn apart, shred by tormenting shred, bleeding out onto Amy's gleaming hardwood floor, staining it.

Dylan ended his call and maintained his stare at Cliff. "I need you and Logan, now." Standing without a second thought, his chair clattered to the floor behind him. Logan did the same, missing the look of alarm on Avery's face as she cradled her stomach.

Questions were thrown across the room and Dylan shut them down with a hand raised in the air. "Listen. I don't have a lot of information. I got a call that someone needs my help and they requested a doctor and someone that can protect the victim. That's all that I know."

"When will they be here?" Amy asked, the question on everyone's mind. There was no other safer place for this person to come than to Carson. The caller must have known this fact, which left Cliff with only a few options running through his mind.

"They are twenty minutes out; just turned off the highway. Cliff, where should we go?"

"My studio. The building upstairs is monitored by my security system and I have sterile equipment at the shop for piercings. Logan can use it."

"Great. Let's go."

Ten minutes later, the three men arrived at Cliff's shop, parking the two vehicles behind the building and using the back entrance. Once they entered, Logan went to work unpacking his travel medical bag and sifting through the sterile cabinet Cliff mentioned to him on the way over. They aren't sure what to expect when the victim arrived, just that there were multiple wounds.

As Cliff reset the security system, Dylan gripped him by the bicep.

"Cliff, I need you to know something before they get here."

"Sure, man. What's up?" Cliff tried to sound casual as he asked, but his pulse pounded differently.

"It is Alexis."

Confused, Cliff replied, "What is?"

"The victim. It is Alexis."

***

Blinking her eyes open, Alexis took in the ripped cloth of the seat pressed against her, then tried her best to turn her head in the other direction, but failed miserably. She was so weak. The last time she felt like this was when she had a bout of the stomach flu eight years ago, nearly rendering her useless for an entire week.

Agonizing pain rippled through her and moan escaped her lips as the car jostled over a bump in the road.

"Sorry. We'll be there soon."

Everything hurt. Alexis mentally took note of her white undershirt stained in red and the tourniquet securely placed on her thigh. She'd lost a lot of blood, too much blood.

"Heath," she groaned in pain, doing all she could to fight against the darkness. Her time was almost up and it was closing in far too quickly.

"Don't you fucking dare, Alexis. Hang on just another few minutes, we're almost there." Her friend turned his head to look at her in the back, and though she couldn't see him well, she knew something must register his alarm because the car jerked as he increased his speed, jostling her in the process

Closing her eyes once more, she settled against the cushion, praying for peace to welcome her.

Whispered words sound close to her ear, offering reassurance as her body was lifted from the car. She barely had a chance to fall back asleep before Heath stopped the car with a jolt, the smell of burnt brakes lingered in the air. Opening her eyes took too much energy, instead she settled against the chest pressed at her side, savoring its warmth. With her face free from the musty seat cushion, Alexis took a deep breath. The smell of spring, freshly cut wood, and water assaulted her senses and Alexis immediately stiffened in the man's arms. Well, as rigid as she could with her blood loss. She recognized that scent, and knew of only one man that wore the Burberry cologne - Cliff.

But what was she doing in Carson? That would mean that Heath drove almost twenty-four hours straight from their post in New Mexico.

"Calm down. You're safe here," Cliff whispered and her muscles relaxed. She knew that Carson was one of the safest places she could be, but she didn't want to endanger the people that she had grown to love, or put Cliff at risk. She could defend herself, but these were simple townspeople.

He carried her through a door at the back of the building. The lights were too bright, causing her to squeeze her eyes tighter, her body flinched in reaction.

"Tell me what we've got," she heard a familiar voice ask. Logan? He was the only doctor in town that she knew, besides Brooks, but the ex-baseball player was a pediatrician.

"Shot through and through to the right shoulder. Bullet hit in the upper portion of her right thigh. It is still lodged in place."

"Fuck," the doctor mumbled before he directed someone else in the room. "Dylan, I need you to gather bags of blood from the medical office. O negative. She's lost a lot and I'm afraid we need it on hand for the surgery. Let's hope the muscles are destroyed."

"What about anesthesia?" Heath asked. She recognized his hand as it gripped hers tightly while Cliff settled her body on a cushioned bed.

"We don't have time. I'll do local anesthesia, but that's the best I can do. If we don't take care of this now, I'm afraid she's going to have an hour or two tops."

Low curses expelled from Heath as Dylan requested where to go at the medical office, promising to return quickly.

Cliff's voice broke through the sounds of metal clanging close to her ear. She assumed it's supplies for the emergency surgery.

"When she comes through this, I want a complete debriefing. But for now, you rest. I'll make sure to get you some clothes too," Cliff voiced in the direction where she heard Heath last.

"Thanks." She listened to the sounds of her friend's feet carrying him out of the room, hopefully to catch some much-needed shuteye. The place won't matter to Heath, she's watched him make camp on the floor of a dirty hotel room, scratchy rug and all.

Alexis jerked as cold fingers probe her shoulder, bringing her back to the moment. These weren't the same gentle fingers that lifted her from the car.

"Shh," a soothing voice whispered in her ear. She wanted so badly to scream, but even that took more energy than she had left.

"I'm going to numb the area on your shoulder, clean it, then stitch it up on both sides."

Her neck stiffened as scissors slid across her skin, removing her shirt from her body. Cliff's inhale of air didn't go unnoticed by Alexis, but she had little time to dwell on his reaction. She imagined that she was covered in purple and black bruises, as well as the dried remains of blood and mud. Logan's fingers swept across her wound and Alexis's mind focused on the pain.

"Cliff, can you hold her head in place? I don't want her to start thrashing. When Dylan returns, I'll have him hold her arms and legs. I'll be able to numb her, but I can't promise that she won't feel any pressure or pain."

Strong hands moved to the sides of her head, but instead of fear or nervousness, Alexis reveled in his soothing touch. Cliff's thumbs stroked back and forth along her hairline and she tried her damnedest to focus on that soothing touch instead of the prick of the needles along her shoulder wound.

Logan was able to clean and stitch the front side of her gash just as heavy footsteps pounded into the room. Dylan had returned with the bags of blood. He helped the men flip her onto her stomach so that Logan could close the wound on the back, the sting of the cool water and antibacterial soap used to clean the exit point was shocking and Alexis clenched her teeth to fight off the throb.

As the men flipped her back over to assess the wound on her leg, Alexis saw stars behind her closed eyelids. The pain was excruciating and the scream she kept buried inside escaped with a flourish. The tourniquet had been doing its job keeping the blood loss as minimal as possible, but as Logan released the tension in the belt around her thigh, all of the nerves in her leg came alive. She could feel every shred of material cut from her leg to expose the wound, every pulse of blood rushing toward her extremities.

The instant Logan's fingers brushed across the ripped skin of her thigh, Alexis' body jerked in response. Dylan held her arms and legs in place, her back arching as she tried to fight off the procedure.

"Shh," Cliff whispered in her ear again, but even the gentle sound of his voice did little to soothe her. Her body was on fire from the ache.

Each poke from the numbing needle felt like a searing stake impaling her skin. Though the nerves around the opening were numb, she could feel every move of muscle, every prod against her bone as Logan searched for the bullet.

Alexis wanted to shout, wanted to yell from the rooftops to tell them to stop, that she couldn't endure the pain any longer. Tears streamed from the corners of her eyes, soaking her hairline.

"I can't take it anymore," Alexis confessed silently.

Her breathing became rushed, erratic. Staccato inhales filled her lungs as she tried to fight off the torture.

"Calm down, Alexis. Please."

Don't they know I can't?

But then gentle strokes wiped away the tears flowing from her eyes and a pair of the softest lips pressed against her forehead. It was the first moment of peace she had felt since she landed in New Mexico months ago. And as the lips pulled away from her head, she tilted back craving their touch again. Wanting the moment of solitude they provided.

Alexis didn't have to wait long. His forehead pressed against hers and calm washed over her. Somehow, some way, she had a connection to Cliff that she'd never experienced before. In the past, she had brushed it off as nothing more than a crush, but what if she had been wrong? He had the power to bring her peace in a time of chaos.

And as he spoke words from a prayer, Alexis hung onto each syllable, each consonant as it glided across her ears, basking in the tranquility. She no longer felt the tension in her leg, or the throbbing of the tugged muscles, or the pinch of her skin as Logan inserted an IV of blood; she only felt the comfort Cliff was providing. And Alexis wished that she could bottle it up and keep it for all time.

She wasn't out of consciousness long, or it didn't appear that way as the hushed voices of her saviors echoed in the space as they talked. Alexis hung onto their every word.

"Her entire team was killed. They were ambushed. Somehow our intel got word to the cartel that we were coming. They never had a chance." That must be Heath explaining the situation.

A voice she recognized as Dylan's piped in. "How did she get out?"

"Using the drone and layouts, I was able to guide her to a false air duct that let out on the side of the bunker. It was the cartel's escape route. She ran about ten miles, taking out five or six men in the process."

"Damn," another voice echoed outside the room.

Something soft brushed against the back of her hand and Alexis pried her eyes open, thankful that the room had been darkened, only a lamp in the corner provided any light. Turning her head, she was surprised to find Cliff resting on his arm beside her, her hand clasped inside his much larger one. Alexis took a moment to drink him in. His massive body cast in soft light and shadows looking just as handsome as she remembered.

He sensed her alertness, his brown eyes popping open in alarm and focusing on her. They stared at each other in silence, but he never ceased the gentle rubbing of his thumb against her skin.

"There was something more though. She was frantic," Heath added in the other room, but Cliff never tore his gaze from her though he had been the one to demand a debrief. "Our team has been ambushed before and she was always the strongest and most reserved. She saw something there that scared her. And we all know Alexis, nothing fazes her."

"But this did," Dylan confirmed.

"We can learn more once she wakes up. Without anything but the over-the-counter meds, she won't be out long."

Cliff's eyes never strayed; his stare penetrated the depths of her soul with every passing second.

"Are you okay?" he whispered, his other hand moved to stroke the top of her head as if he needed to verify himself that she was across from him.

She tried to answer, but a muffled noise crawled from her lips.

"You don't have to answer. Just shake your head."

Alexis nods, more or less just happy to be alive.

"Good. I'll get some water and let everyone knew that you're awake."

Her terror spiked and she instinctively squeezed his hand. "Don't. Leave. Me." The words come out scratchy and nothing more than a whisper.

"Okay. I'll stay." Cliff never removed his hand from hers, but he used the rolling seat he'd taken residence on and leaned out toward the hallway. That's when she realized that she was in his tattoo shop.

"Guys. Can I get a cup of water? She's waking up."

A thundering of feet stomped across the floor as the men made their way toward her. She tried not to flinch as the group approached, but Cliff caught her motion and rested his other hand back on her head.

"Small sips," Logan told her as he handed her a cup of water with a straw, his usually slicked back hair in disarray. Of course, Alexis was confident that she had better looking days as well. That was the moment when she remembered the men having to cut her clothing free from her body. Alexis glanced down to find herself draped in a heavy blanket, thankful for the covering.

"Better?" Logan asked as he pulled the straw free from her mouth.

"Thanks," she replied, her voice no louder than before, but the dryness tolerable.

They gazed at her in silence and Alexis wondered if they were preparing for her to fight or take flight. Fortunately for them, with her hand securely wrapped in Cliff's, she had no desire to go anywhere.

It only took Dylan and Heath a few short minutes before they begin probing her for more information and she relayed to them everything she remembered during the time that she was inside the bunker.

"What had you startled toward the end?" Heath queried. "When you went to get the chair from the first room, I heard your gasp. What did you see?"

Licking her lips, Alexis could feel Cliff's body tremble in her hold. It was something that she'd have to delve into later. "A group of men brought in a woman.

Most likely one that they planned to break and use for trafficking. But then a last man entered."

"Did you recognize him?" Cliff asked from beside her.

"Yes, he was. . .well, he was my father."

The silence was deafening. Alexis never understood that expression until that moment. She wanted someone to say something, to say anything before the quiet threatened to suffocate her.

"This makes so much sense," Dylan replied as he examined something on his phone, Heath leaning over his shoulder to get a better look.

"What does?" Cliff and Logan ask at the same time.

"She's been pulled from the FBI records. They know she's now a target for the cartel," Heath pointed out. "We didn't understand why until just now."

Dylan quickly added, "And it means if they can get information, they'll offer her up on a platter to these men."

A growl filled the room and Alexis cocked her head toward the noise and found that Cliff's face turned a deep shade of red.

"I won't let that happen," he snarled and the men in the room nodded in agreement.

"Absolutely not. We're going to get this all figured out. But first, Alexis needs to rest in a safe place."

"She'll stay with me," her savior commanded, but Heath shook his head. "I'm not sure living above a tattoo shop is very conspicuous. I'm certain that they'll trace her to this location at some point."

"You're right. I'm taking her to my cabin."

While Logan busied himself tugging the IV free from her arm, his head jerked up at Cliff's announcement. "I didn't know that you had a cabin."

"Exactly. And there should be no doubt that I have the skills to protect her as well."

Not a single one disagreed.

Alexis breathed a sigh of relief at the arrangement and while Logan finished dressing her wounds, they scheduled a time for everyone to meet at the banquet room at Angie's Diner the next day. Collectively they would need to come up with a plan, not only to protect Alexis but to keep the cartel from infiltrating their town in their haste to find her.

"I need to run upstairs real quick to grab a few things. I'll be right back," Cliff explained before he pressed a kiss to her forehead. "Watch her," he added to the men before releasing her hand. She immediately felt his absence.

Heath settled in his vacated seat and examined her closely. "You know, for two people that have been together only a handful of times, you both seem very close to each other."

"I know. . .I can't explain it." How could she? Since the moment he shook her hand almost three years ago she knew that Cliff was someone important.

"Just be careful, Alexis. I can protect you physically, but I can't protect you from a broken heart."

Heath was being the older brother figure she never had, but he didn't need to worry about her feelings, she never stayed in a place long enough to grow attachments.

A few minutes later, Cliff came barreling down a stairwell and back into the room carrying multiple black duffle bags. She could only guess what contents reside inside. He approached her with a smaller bag and unzipped it before resting it on the table, revealing gray cotton.

"I figured you'd want something clean to wear. It's a pair of sweatpants and a T-shirt. They probably won't fit. Sorry," he rambles and Alexis places her hand on his holding the bag, a spark fizzing up her arm at the contact.

"Thank you." She risked a smile and her heart soared as he bashfully returned it.

Knowing she wanted privacy, the men left the room allowing her to change. But attempting to unhook her bra became too much to handle and Alexis cried out in pain.

Cliff entered the room first, Heath hot on his heels, but her best friend immediately turned around when he saw that she was clad in a blood-stained sports bra and panties.

"Let me help you," Cliff whispered as he walked toward her. "It may be easiest to cut the bra free so you don't put pressure on your wound." At her nod, he lifted a pair of scissors from the counter and made three cuts. One on each strap and the other down the back. The material pooled on the floor and she used her good arm to cover her breasts.

Reaching into the bag for the T-shirt, Cliff held it over her head and tugged it down. "Never imagined that this would be how I'd get you naked the first time." Her body shuddered at his claim.

"How. . .how did you imagine it happening?" Alexis asked as she slipped her arms through the holes of the shirt, the deep V of the neckline dipping between her breasts.

"Well, you wouldn't have been on the brink of death. That's for sure." Chuckling to himself as he twisted the bottom of the shirt into a knot at her waist, he added, "I'd probably like to kiss you first. But I guess beggars can't be choosers, huh?"

"Probably not. But you can kiss me now. If you want, that is." Alexis had never spoken so boldly before, not when it was in her personal life. She spent her days bossing her teammates around, she liked to spend her off-hours more submissive.

"I can't," he told her and Alexis felt herself shrink in size. Of course, this gorgeous man with the mesmerizing tattoos snaking up his arms wouldn't want her when she looks like this – death warmed over. "If I hurt you at all, it would kill me. I couldn't risk that."

At least he gives a good reason.

"I'm assuming you want your underwear gone too?"

At her nod, he slipped the scissors on both sides of her hips, slicing the material apart and landing between her feet. The once white material now a shade of dark red. Alexis didn't miss Cliff's gasp as he took in the cotton and the residual blood on her legs.

"I'm so sorry, sweetheart."

Alexis peered over her shoulder and found Cliff crouched with the sweatpants spread wide for her to step inside, his gaze trained to the floor. Alexis imagined that he was trying to be respectful of her lower body being bare before him. Then again, she probably reeked as well. It had been four days since she showered.

"You don't have to apologize. I stink."

His head snapped up toward her in attention. "I don't like seeing you hurt."

"Oh," she whispered, taking a step back into one of the legs of the sweatpants, then braced herself against the bed to lift her injured leg a few inches, allowing Cliff to slip the material under her foot.

"Thank you," she told him as he rolled the waistband a few times so they sit at her hips.

"You're welcome. Let's get you out of here and I'll make you something to eat." Immediately her stomach responded with an angry growl at the notion of food. "On second thought, maybe I should have someone grab something from Angie's and bring it over."

"No, worries," Logan piped in, hollering from around the door jamb. "Mama Connelly is bringing food over to your place."

"How does she know where I have a cabin?"

She watched Logan's face transform as if Cliff had asked the dumbest question known to man.

"Dude, she knows everything. Don't act so surprised."

"I'm guessing that means everyone will be coming along?" Cliff asked, and the thought of everyone seeing her in this haphazard state sent a shiver down her spine, she found herself seeking out Cliff's hand.

"Naw, they'll wait until tomorrow. But be prepared for Amy to go all motherly on you, Alexis."

She did love Mrs. Connelly. It was hard not to. When Alexis first arrived in Carson, Mrs. Connelly went out of her way to make sure that Alexis found a place to stay and that it felt like home. Those first three days she witnessed what a true family could look like.

"I'm sure I can manage."

Together they all filed out of the building, Cliff took special care with her as she hobbled due to the shoulder and leg restraint Logan affixed to her body. He slid the passenger seat of his truck as far back as it would go and gestured for her to enter. A whimper escaped her lips as she tried to bend at the hips to get comfortable and Cliff had to pluck her off the ground and settle her in the seat himself.

"I'm sorry, sweetheart. You can rest when we get home."

Home. Such a novel thought, but Alexis hadn't called a place home since she was a little girl. Just the prospect of staying in the place that made Cliff feel safest thrilled her. Because if it was good enough for the man that set her blood on fire, then it would be good enough for her.

Chapter Three

It didn't take long for Alexis' head to droop as exhaustion claimed her. Cliff tried to keep his eyes on the road, but he failed miserably. His attention was one hundred percent focused on Alexis. It was still early in the evening, Alexis' surgery lasting through the night, and the brightness of the afternoon drifted behind the mountains surrounding their town, leaving the sky a darkening blue.

As Cliff drove down the road, he noticed people drifted out onto their porches, lights flicked on as he passed, everyone tossed a welcoming wave toward him. This was one of his favorite things about the town, the friendliness everyone provided without question.

He wondered how many people knew of Alexis' return. The lady Busy Bees were infamous for figuring out things in the town that no one else knew. Hell, they knew of his cabin purchase before he had even signed on the dotted line. They were an intel team that Cliff wanted to study and figure out all of their secrets.

The car hit a divot in the road, jostling their bodies back and forth as it settled back on the surface.

Cliff jerked his head toward his passenger, alarm over hurting her surged through his body.

"Sorry," he murmured as she groaned as she readjusted her body again.

"That's okay." She moved again in the seat, her face tightening with each change until she found a more comfortable position. Her eyes skim across the fields on the sides of the road as they ventured further away from Carson's center. He could tell the moment fright gripped her. What little strength she had stiffened her spine and Alexis' hand grabbed the handle on the door. Even in the dimness of the vehicle, Cliff could make out the white of her knuckles. Her lack of trust and faith in him was disheartening.

 "Don't worry, we're not that far out. Logan and Dylan are right behind us," he pointed out, trying to ease her fear. She nodded once, but her back stayed ram-rod straight. It had been a long time since Cliff felt the desire to put someone at ease, the thought didn't come naturally to him in most instances, but with Alexis, he had it in spades.

"I can take you somewhere else, Alexis. You don't have to stay with me." Cliff didn't want her to feel unsafe with him – protection was what he wanted to give her. And not just protection from her father. He wanted to protect her from the world for the rest of her days.

His heart raced at the premonition of losing her before he even had her. Turning his gaze back toward the road, Cliff was determined to do what was best for Alexis, even if that meant handing her to someone else. As expected, thoughts of Alexis wrapped in the arms of another had Cliff gripping the steering wheel with such a fierceness he was afraid he'd bend it.

A feather-light touch on his arm jolted his gaze away from the road and onto his body. Alexis' hand gently rested on his forearm, her thumb rubbing small circles on the dragon scales of his tattoo. Flutters erupted in his chest. In the spot where he was certain his demolished heart had resided years before. Maybe he had been wrong all these years. Maybe his heart was just waiting for the right moment to come alive.

"I want to stay with you. I feel safe with you."

Cliff nodded once, turning his attention back to the road, expecting his abrupt reaction to turn her away. But as expected, she surprised him. Her small hand continued to rest on his arm. Her palms weren't delicate or soft, the calluses and rough patches scraped against his skin. Alexis was no meek or mild woman, she could easily hold her own against any man, that Cliff was certain. Which left him wondering what it was about these men and her father that had her spooked.

The cabin came into view in the distance off in the distance and Alexis' grip on his arm tightened.

"I know this place."

He tried to act surprised as he asked, "Really?" Of course, she wouldn't know that he had seen her here before.

"Yeah, when Dylan's brother-in-law, Austin, was being blackmailed and they asked for my help, I found this path. I ran it almost every day. I always thought that this cabin was adorable. It just needed some tender loving care, you know?"

For some reason, hearing Alexis say something was adorable didn't fit her personality. She was a ninja-like badass after all, but maybe that was just the persona she showed the world. Cliff couldn't wait to learn her more feminine side and he was going to do everything in his power to discover more.

"I used to come here to unwind, especially when I had flashbacks from the war and some of the terrible things that I've seen. Not many people knew that I bought this cabin. I've been spending my free time fixing it up. So, it is far from perfect, but it is livable."

"I'm sure it is great." He heard her voice change as she smiled, a bit of excitement tingeing each word.

The truck eased into a spot beside the house, Logan and Dylan pulled their vehicles into the open spots beside them. Cliff jumped out of the vehicle and shook his head toward the men as they climbed free from their cars.

"It is okay, guys. I can take her inside and get her settled," he explained, but both men shook their heads.

"While I have no doubts that you can, I'm certain Logan wants to check her vitals one last time."

Crossing his arms against his chest, he cocked an eyebrow at his friend. Cliff stared down at Dylan. "And what's your excuse?"

"Maybe I don't trust you." Dylan shrugged his shoulders as if that was a viable reason, as false as it may be.

"You and I both knew that isn't the case."

"Well, maybe I just want to make sure that *she* trusts you."

Cliff found that more believable. Especially since Dylan, Logan, and Heath witnessed the connection he and Alexis had when she was brought into his shop. It was something that he couldn't explain then or now.

Ignoring his friends, Cliff moved around the vehicle and opened the door on the passenger side, easily lifting Alexis into his arms. She tried to argue and squirm against his hold, but one steely glance in her direction ended her fight quickly.

As he maneuvered her across the porch and toward the entry, his mind traveled back to the past where he wanted to carry his wife over the threshold of their apartment after eloping. But she didn't want any of that, she was determined to be his equal and not show an ounce of relenting toward him treating her like the prized treasure she was.

To Cliff, it felt surreal to create that moment with this particular woman – he had to remember that Alexis was nothing like his ex. Her stare penetrated the side of his face, the skin burned as if singed by fire. Her attention was that potent to him. He took a second to glance down at her, their eyes locking as he crossed the threshold leading to his home.

Time stood still as they lost themselves in the moment. It was only the two of them as the world drifted away. He wondered if she felt the significance of this moment.

The spell was broken as Logan's hushed voice reached Cliff's ears. "I feel like we're encroaching on a special moment."

"Shut up," Dylan replied to him. A grunt quickly followed and Cliff assumed that Logan was at the receiving end of Dylan's fist.

Continuing past the kitchen, Cliff walked into the small, but comfortable living room, depositing Alexis carefully on the couch. She winced as he settled her legs against the cushion, whispering an apology as he tucked a pillow under her head.

Lifting a finger in the direction of his friends, Cliff barked, "You have five minutes while I go make sure the bedroom is ready for her. And before you ask, I plan on sleeping on the couch. She will take the bed."

With one final glance over his shoulder, Cliff watched as Logan approached Alexis, his medicine bag in hand. Down a narrow hallway, Cliff entered his bedroom. The space was small, just enough for a queen-sized mattress and a dresser, but that's all he needed. He can see how cramped it may seem to a woman.

Ripping the sheets from his bed, he rolled them in his arms and tossed the ball of cotton on the floor, the stark white of the sheets was a deep contrast to the dark stain of the wood floors. Grabbing a clean set from a shelf in the closet, Cliff quickly made the bed and replaced the duvet.

Bending down, he lifted the balled-up sheets into his arms and headed back down the hallway, stopping first to make sure that his bathroom was tidy. Despite his razor and shaving cream on the counter, it was clean enough. Years overseas in the Army taught him to take pleasure in a clean space. He did his best to maintain it.

After throwing the laundry in the washer and starting a cycle, Cliff made his way back out to the living room where Logan was closing the latch on his bag.

"She's going to need help changing the dressings on her shoulder and thigh. It's going to take a few days before she can put more pressure on her leg. Little to no walking unless it is with the crutches I'm going to bring by tomorrow." Cliff nodded, but Logan turned his attention back toward Alexis. "I mean it."

"Fine," she grumbled and Cliff smiled for the first time since she arrived at his shop. They both knew she's going to do whatever she could to get moving around.

Cliff's pocket began to vibrate and he fished his phone free finding a security alert at his cabin. But instead of a grimace, he smiled broadly at the group.

"It seems Mama Connelly couldn't wait any longer. She's pulling up as we speak."

"She can't see me like this!" Alexis fretted, her body moved as she tried to sit up, but then her face immediately turned white. Cliff imagined the blinding pain became too much.

"You look beautiful. Now, stay still," he commanded, his smile returning as she settled back down against the cushions.

It was not long before a knock sounded on his front door and Dylan moved to answer for him. Amy Connelly was no threat and Cliff would much rather stay by Alexis' side.

Rushing through the entry and right over to the couch, Mrs. Connelly knocked Cliff out of the way and kneeled beside Alexis, taking her hand. "Oh, you poor dear. I heard what happened and I was just so frightened for you. You must have been so scared."

"I'm okay, Mrs. Connelly. I've been through worse," Alexis tried to explain, but by Amy's expression, she was having none of it.

"Now, don't you go lying to me, young lady. It is not every day you get chased down by a drug cartel that happens to be run by your father."

Everyone in the room grew quiet, the only sound Cliff could make out was that of his teeth grinding together. No one was supposed to know that Alexis was here.

"Amy. . ." Dylan began, but Mrs. Connelly quickly hushed him.

"Don't you worry about how I got my information. I have my ways. The Lady Busy Bees have nothing on me, my dear boys. But you don't have to worry, only people of importance will know."

Dylan groaned loud enough to earn him a devilish glare from his mother-in-law. "Which means the entire town knows."

Standing, Amy rested her hands on her hips looking exactly like a mother of six would as she prepared to scold one of her children. "Of course, they do. How else do you expect us to protect her? It wasn't too long ago you needed our assistance, don't forget what we're capable of, young man." Watching the fiery gaze in Amy's eyes had Cliff realizing one particular thing. He wasn't scared of much in this world, but being on the receiving end of Amy's wrath sent trickles of fear down his spine. It was amazing.

Dylan quickly apologized, "Yes, ma'am. You're right."

Her expression quickly morphed back into that of a doting mother as Amy turned her gaze back toward Alexis. "Of course, I'm right. Women usually are. You'd think he'd have learned this by now. Maybe I need to have a talk with Sydney. Which reminds me, everyone will be meeting here tomorrow."

Cliff looked around the small space wondering how everyone would fit, just as Amy added, "Don't worry. It will be a lovely day tomorrow; we can all go outside if need be. And we're all bringing a dish so if anyone happens to be on the bad side of things, they'll think we're just having a cookout and housewarming party."

Cliff shook his head knowing that Mrs. Connelly would have come prepared with a grand scheme to fool anyone not on the up-and-up.

"Logan, dear, please put my bag in the kitchen. I brought soup for Alexis and the meatloaf special from Angie's for Cliff."

He wanted to kiss that woman. She brought his favorite meal.

"Thank you, Mrs. Connelly."

"Of course. Now, I'll be heading back home. I left Joseph burning some cardboard boxes in the backyard, and knowing the pyromaniac in him, I'm going to go home to half of the yard burnt to a crisp."

Everyone, including Alexis, laughed at her joke. "At least as fire chief, he'll be able to put it out quickly," Alexis added.

"Very true. Good night all."

Mrs. Connelly left just as quickly as she came. Dylan and Logan were not far behind, leaving Alexis and Cliff lingering in the living room alone for the first time since she arrived.

A quiet tension filled every empty space in the room. From across the space their eyes met, and Cliff held his breath, too afraid that their moment would be broken. Why had this woman affected him so? What kind of spell did she place on him all those years ago that left him craving her? He wanted an answer, needed one, but just the thought of her not being as affected by him left a bitter taste in his mouth.

"So. . ." Alexis whispered from her residence on the couch and Cliff immediately regretted staying silent for so long. He probably made her feel uncomfortable and that wasn't something he ever wanted her to feel with him.

"Sorry. I can. . .ugh. . .heat up the food for you."

A small smile slowly blossomed on her lips transforming her face and Cliff felt his heart jerk in response. He couldn't help but think that he needed to get a better handle on his emotions around Alexis or his natural instincts to protect her would fall by the wayside.

"That sounds great. Thanks. And then, maybe you can help me figure out how to take a shower?"

Of course, she would want to get clean. He can't even imagine the last time she had a chance to bathe. And after being hurt, Cliff imagined that she wanted all the dirt and grime off of her skin. But he only knew one way to help her do that without her hurting herself, he just hoped that he could control himself long enough to not cross any lines.

"Yeah, I can help you do that," he told her as he walked into his galley-style kitchen, popping the glass bowl containing her soup in the microwave. It took just a few minutes, but he carried the container to the living room and placed it on the end table beside his sofa. With a soft touch and a few curses from Alexis, he helped move her into a sitting position. A quick trip back into the kitchen to heat up his own meal, Cliff joined her on the couch and they ate in companionable silence. But in Cliff's mind, images of a naked Alexis ran through his mind. Like before, he knew he couldn't let his stare linger on her body. He was too much of a gentleman for that. He wanted to relish seeing her bare to him the first time if they ever get to a more intimate part of their relationship. And until her father was caught, Cliff needed to keep those plans to himself.

"Can you help me up?" a voice whispered beside him and Cliff startled. He had been lost in his thoughts and as his fork clinked against his plate, he realized that he had finished eating his meal without savoring a single bite.

Cliff gathered his plate and her bowl, walked briskly to the kitchen to deposit the items in the sink, then he hurried his way back to Alexis.

"Alright, up you go," he explained as he leaned toward her, placing an arm behind her back and thighs, and easily lifted her in his hold. The corner of his mouth tilted upward as she released a small sigh.

Flipping the switch in the bathroom with his elbow, he bathed the space in light. White penny tiles lined the floor and met the white marble tile in the shower. A navy-blue vanity with more white marble stood across from him and he moved to deposit Alexis on the surface. She flinched as he set her down, but she didn't complain.

"If you want, I can call one of the girls to come to help you bathe." He hoped that she understood the other option of him assisting her in the shower. Cliff wanted Alexis to know that she always has a choice, he'd never make that decision for her. But she surprised him as her eyes narrowed and lips pursed, her good hand gripped the lip of the counter as if to break off a piece of the stone.

"I don't want one of your women to wash me," she said through clenched teeth and Cliff had never seen jealousy look so beautiful until that second.

He tried not to chuckle, but one escaped anyway. "I just meant that I could call one of the Connelly sisters to help. Harlan and Cassidy live just down the road."

"Oh," she blushed, a beautiful rose color rose on her tanned cheeks.

Lifting her chin with the side of his bent index finger, Cliff paused until she brought her eyes to meet his. "I would never put you in a position like that, Alexis, and I hate that you think that I would. I realize now that we knew very little about each other, but I can't deny the reaction I have when I'm near you. I want to possess all of you, but only when you're ready to give yourself to me."

Her eyes flicked back and forth between Cliff's, but he waited patiently for her response. It took just a few beats until she replied. "You're right and I'm sorry. I want to know you better. I want to know all of you and I've never felt like this about anyone so quickly."

"Don't worry, we'll take our time. I need to make sure that you're safe first. And I may not be a saint, but believe me when I say that there isn't a single woman that can hold a candle to you."

"Wow," she whispered, leaning closer to him. He wanted to kiss her, needed it more than his next breath, but took a retreating step back instead. She was not ready for him yet despite her words.

"Let's get you in the shower, okay?" Cliff reached around his back and gripped the cotton of his T-shirt, tugging the material over his head without much effort. He tried not to smile at the surprised gasp he heard from Alexis. Despite the bullet scars and tattoos Cliff knew that his body was in peak shape. His shoes, socks, and pants quickly followed, the pile on the floor growing with each piece.

Moving back toward Alexis's perch on the vanity, Cliff reached out and applied soft pressure on her ankles. Against his fingers, he could feel her pulse spike.

"Okay, sweetheart. Your turn."

***

Alexis didn't know what came over her. She was so used to being the strong independent type, living up to her nickname of ninja, that allowing herself to be vulnerable seemed foreign. It wasn't that she never wanted to let someone else take care of her, it was more that she had never had the opportunity. But something about Cliff was different. With him, she wanted to let her hair down, she wanted to let him ease her pain. This man that she'd met only a few times but felt like he knew her darkest secrets before she even uttered her name.

Was this how it was supposed to be?

Alexis had so many questions, but they completely fell to the wayside as Cliff's fingers inched up her legs. He delicately removed the brace around her thigh, doing the same with the support holding her injured arm. His hand gently brushed her hair to the side as he slipped the Velcro free from the latch.

She could feel his anger rise as she winced involuntarily at the movement.

"I'm, ugh, not sure I will be able to tolerate the water on my wounds."

"That's okay. You can sit on the bench and I'll help you," Cliff explained as he delicately maneuvered the shirt off her body. The movement had Alexis biting back a cry of pain. "Sorry," he quickly apologized.

Gritting her teeth, she replied, "Not your fault," but Cliff just shook his head.

Gently he lifted her hips up from the counter, his gaze trained to the task at hand and not her bare breasts a mere few inches away from his face. The pants pulled off her bottom easily but got caught on some of the tape surrounding the dressing of her leg wound.

"We should probably take these off and put on a clean set."

"Cliff?" she prompted as he murmured to himself, his fingers lightly tugging away the adhesive of the dressing. "Cliff?" she said again and he finally looked up at her.

"Why are you doing this?"

Alexis couldn't help herself from asking the question. It had been plaguing her since she felt lifted in his arms in the darkness of the night. He willingly brought her to his refuge and she wanted to understand why.

His eyes latched onto hers immediately. "Doing what?"

"This," she gestured around with her good hand, not even caring that the sweatpants were dangling at her ankles. "Helping me, protecting me, taking care of me."

Alexis needed to know his motives. Did he just want to get in her pants? Did he feel the same attraction to her that she felt toward him? Did he feel obligated?

And as the seconds ticked by, she felt the weight of his hesitancy on her shoulders.

"It was what anyone would do," he replied, immediately crushing what little hope Alexis had left. She'd been let down her entire life, what made her think that this man was any different?

The room grew quiet again, the only sound was her heartbeat pounding in her ears as Cliff removed the gauze on her wounds. She didn't feel the pull of her skin or the feel of Cliff's touch. All Alexis felt was the overwhelming sting of rejection.

"Okay. I think we're ready." Cliff's voice broke through and Alexis' eyes followed his retreating backside over to the shower.

Defiantly she jumped down from the counter, wincing as she landed on her good leg. "I can handle this by myself. Thanks," she told him, jumping on one leg until she reached the shower. Thank goodness for years of yoga improving her balance.

But her balance was nothing against the sneer Cliff sent her way as she bounced his way. "Don't," he growled.

"I'm very capable," she retorted, wishing she could cross her arms against her chest, but she was already growing lightheaded from her movements. Alexis began rethinking her idea.

"You have been shot, went through two bags of blood, and are turning the same color as the tiles on the floor. Let me help you."

"I'm not a charity case for you!" she yelled, and as she watched Cliff's face turn red, she imagined if this was a cartoon steam would billow from his ears.

"No, you're not. You're fucking important!" he shouted back in return, his chest rising up and down with his jagged breaths.

Alexis couldn't argue with him now. Even though she wanted to ask to whom she was important, but the caregiver at her last group home always told her to never poke a bear. She never understood that saying until this moment. And Cliff seemed like a bear that had been poked one too many times.

She knew she should apologize for her irrational reaction. Hell, she even had the excuse of the injury and blood loss to blame, but she couldn't bring herself to say the words. Alexis was stubborn through and through.

But Cliff brought it upon himself to express his regret first, surprising her. With a hand on the back of his neck, he contritely stared at the floor as he said, "Look, I'm sorry that I yelled. I want to help you. I wouldn't have agreed for anyone else."

Her head bobbed once in agreement as she reached out with her free hand to grip his shoulder. Effortlessly he guided her into the shower, sitting down on the bench first, then guiding her between his legs. Alexis was thankful that he kept the boxer briefs on his body because she wasn't sure how she would have reacted had she felt his naked body against hers.

"We'll wash your body with the antibacterial soap first, then we can do your hair, okay?" he asked her in a soft voice, and she wondered if he was struggling with their proximity as much as she was.

Whispering her reply, "Okay," Alexis allowed him to rub the lathered washcloth over her skin, only relenting the material to her to cleanse the area between her legs. His touch was clinical in nature and she wondered how many times he may have done this for someone else. She knew enough about his military background but none of his childhood. That information was locked up tightly somewhere.

As much as the warm water stung her wounds, she took pleasure in the thought of wiping away the last few days. Killing people was part of her job, but she hated how she felt afterward. Alexis understood how Lady Macbeth felt in Shakespeare's play, that she could never wash the blood from his hands, dyeing the waters red instead. Of course, she always thought the character was a bit crazy. Maybe she was too.

"Ready for your hair?" His voice was rough behind her and she wondered how difficult it was for him to keep his body in check.

"Yeah," she whispered.

Moving around her effortlessly, he stood and grabbed a handheld showerhead, then twisted her body so that she sat sideways on the bench.

Bending his knees, he knelt on the shower floor, his large body filled the space. Cliff's head inched closer to her until his lips were just a breath away from her ear. "Tilt your head back."

She complied as Cliff held the showerhead over her hair, wetting her long dark tresses. Alexis closed her eyes, only opening them when she heard a clink on the floor, but quickly closed them again as Cliff's hands massaged and lathered her hair with shampoo.

"Sorry if it is too manly. It is all that I have. I can grab you some at the store; just tell me what you like."

She was shocked at the sound of nervousness in his voice as if his shampoo wasn't good enough for her.

"Thank you, Cliff. This shampoo is fine. Maybe just some conditioner, if you don't mind?"

His answering chuckle was like a ray of sunshine after a storm. Her heart burst with joy knowing she caused his spark of happiness.

"You're in luck," he told her. "I have some."

Sitting up, she looked over at him suspiciously. "Really?"

Cliff shrugged his shoulders as if an ex-Army Ranger and tattoo artist using conditioner for his hair was a likely occurrence. "I like the way it makes my hair look. And it's easier to comb after a shower."

"Mmhmm."

"Lean back. We're almost done."

Cliff washed the rest of the trying two days away until she was left feeling fresh and new. He reached for a towel tucked into a cabinet and patted down her body, then draped it around his waist before reaching out for another towel and wrapping it around her shoulders.

Lifting her in his arms, he carried her through the hall and into a small but clean bedroom where he eased her onto the mattress. With a similar skill to Logan's, Cliff applied ointment to her wounds then redressed them, the sutures stung as they pulled at her skin.

"Sorry," he mumbled. "Logan said you should be feeling better in a few days, just take it easy, okay? I'm going to help you get dressed and let you get some sleep."

He stalked over to his dresser, tugged out a navy blue T-shirt and a pair of plaid boxer shorts. It was exactly what she would be wearing if she was at her home. Except, she didn't really have a home, just a studio apartment she rented for cheap close to the office. That way, if she got a call late at night or early in the morning, she could get there sooner.

As he had done at his tattoo studio, he lifted her arms and legs into the clothing, only satisfied when she was completely covered up.

"I'm going to put the compression wrap back on your leg, but I think you can do without the sling tonight or are you a mover while you sleep?"

"Um. . .I don't know," she told him bashfully. Alexis had never been one to share her bed with anyone, so she was unable to answer that question truthfully. She liked her privacy and never felt a special connection with someone to bring them to her apartment.

"Okay. Well, how about we go without it at first, but if I think you need it when I check on you, we'll put it back on."

She ignored his suggestion, instead Alexis focused on the fact that he was laying her down in his bed, tucking the duvet that smelled like him under her chin. "I feel terrible kicking you out of your bed."

"Don't be. I never get much sleep anyway."

Curious, Alexis asked, "Why is that? Nightmares?" She had heard some horror stories of men struggling with PTSD after the war. To her, it made perfect sense that Cliff would experience those same tormenting thoughts.

"No."

"Then why?" she pressed.

His chest heaved with a sigh as he stepped toward the door; the only light in the space was that from the bathroom down the way, his large body now blocking it. She wished that she could see his expression.

"Loneliness."

"Thank you, Cliff."

He grunted in response, closing the door behind him. The room was bathed in darkness and Alexis hated not having the opportunity to look around the room. She wanted to know more about Cliff. What made him tick? What made him smile? Did he keep things to remind himself of a memory? Alexis wanted to know it all. But the weight of her eyelids became too heavy and she could no longer fight against the desire to give into sleep. She always had tomorrow.

A scream startled her from sleep and her eyes popped open looking around the room in horror. Until she realized the noise was coming from her own throat. Unexpectedly the door to the bedroom opened and Cliff rushed inside. Without any light, Alexis couldn't see the fear in his expression, but she knew that it was there. It was the way he gently caressed her arms and face to make sure nothing on her was harmed. His thumb wiped away wetness from her cheek and it was the first time Alexis realized that she has been crying.

"Bad dream?" he asked in a hushed voice, and Alexis nodded not knowing if he could see her.

"I keep seeing images of faceless girls being taken away by men, men like my father. And I couldn't stop him."

"We can and we will. Don't worry, we're going to solve this and keep you safe at the same time."

"Seems impossible," she grumbled as she settled back against the pillow.

"It is not, trust me. I've dealt with men like this before."

"Probably not when the stakes are this high, or you have something he wanted."

"And what's that?"

"Me."

Cliff grew silent then, Alexis wondered if he finally realized the weight of what she had brought to all of them. If she was of a better mind, she would up and leave first thing in the morning, but something inside her screamed that Cliff wasn't going to let that happen on his watch.

Trust him, he had asked and Alexis wondered if that was something she could do at all. Trust.

Cliff turned his body and sat on the edge of the bed, one of his hands weaving through his hair. She wanted to do the same, offer him comfort by the stroke of her hand, but she knew she wasn't in that position. She assumed he planned on going back out to the bedroom, but after a minute passed with his gaze trained down the hall, Alexis' curiosity piqued.

"What are you doing?"

"Waiting for you to fall asleep," his strained voice replied.

"You could. . .ugh. . .sleep here with me. I mean, it is silly for you to sleep on the couch at your own home."

Cliff's head jerked her way and Alexis almost jumped at the feral gaze in his eyes. Even in the blackness, she could make out the ferocity in the irises.

"I haven't shared a bed with someone in a very *very* long time." His voice was pained as if remembering a nightmare of his own – one from his past.

"That's okay. Neither have I. Please? It may keep the dreams away." She knew she was throwing out the big punches. Cliff was the kind of man that would bend over backward for someone that he cared about – she knew this about him already. She remembered how he came out, literally guns locked and loaded when they first met. He was prepared to do whatever he needed to save someone he considered a friend.

Wordlessly, Cliff skirted around the bed until he stood on the other side. The duvet lifted and she instantly felt the change in heat as he slipped under the covers. Alexis started to consider that this maybe wasn't the best decision she'd made. How was she ever going to get to sleep now with this beautiful man lying beside her with intricate tattoos on his arms and chest that she wanted to trace with her tongue? Yes, this was definitely the worst decision she'd ever made.

"Go to sleep," he growled, his arms on top of the covers and folded against his chest.

With a gentle smile, Alexis turned her head until it once again was facing the ceiling and closed her eyes. "Good night, Cliff. Sweet dreams."

It was early when Alexis woke the next morning. Not quite bright enough for sunlight, but just light enough that she could make out the empty bed next to her. Even though she conned Cliff into sleeping in the bed with her during the night, she slept the rest of the night wonderfully. Maybe the notion that he was there to protect her helped put her mind at ease.

Gingerly slipping out of bed, Alexis was surprised to find a pair of crutches resting against the nightstand. She didn't recall them being there the night before, but maybe that was why Cliff was out of bed.

Regardless of her desire to inspect everything in the room, Alexis gripped the crutches, placed them under her arms, and began to maneuver through the house. In the living room, she stopped suddenly.

How did she miss this yesterday?

Her only thought was that she was too out of it to recognize the image in the picture. There were several scattered across the wall, all of varying places in Carson that Alexis recognized. But she knew those fingers anywhere. That day she had gone for a run on this path surrounding Cliff's cabin, she stopped to catch her breath and had gently run her fingers over the top of the wheat stalks. For this image to be so crisp and clear would mean that the photographer had been very close to her body.

When Cliff pulled into the cabin's drive yesterday, Alexis' tried not to let on how much she adored this place. She had been hoping that if she ever retired from her duties that she could escape here away from everyone. This would be the place Alexis would lay down roots. Now, she realized that Cliff felt the same.

Inspecting each of the portraits on the wall, Alexis' eyes traveled toward the mantle above the fireplace. The space was pretty bare, only sparsely decorated with a few odds and ends, but lying face down was a small picture. Lifting the image, a cheerful woman smiled back at her. Alexis found herself returning the gesture. Her pale blonde hair flew around her face on a breeze and the hem of her dress did the same around her tanned legs. She was beautiful, but strangely, Alexis felt not an ounce of jealousy. Whoever this woman was, Cliff had carried this picture close with him. The edges of the photograph were worn, the font itself scraped and tattered. Alexis couldn't help but think that this picture held more than just a memory for Cliff.

Feeling like she had invaded his privacy, Alexis placed the picture back exactly how she found it and then hobbled around the couch toward the kitchen. She was surprised to find it empty as well. Considering the nature of the photos in the room, Alexis took a chance to check outside the cabin.

It took some skill to open and hold the door ajar while gripping the crutches, but she managed. Standing on the front porch, she glanced around the open field, the same one as the picture, but couldn't locate Cliff. Alexis thought back to her time running along the path and remembered access to a lake behind the cabin.

Gritting her teeth, Alexis teetered down the steps then slowly made her way toward a narrow opening in the tree line. She followed the trail for a while until the cabin was no longer in view behind her and for a moment, Alexis worried that she would be unable to make it back. Her weakness grew with each step and her vision clouded with white.

Leaning against a large tree, Alexis took a minute to rest, thankful when her vision returned. And though she was not at full strength, she felt ten times better after the break. She just hoped that she was getting close because it would take her an hour to make it back up the small hill.

Finally, an opening broke through the forest and the lake came into view. At first, Alexis didn't see Cliff, but turning her attention to the left, she found a lone dock perched over the water and a man sitting on the edge – looking just as lost as she felt.

Chapter Four

Cliff tried his hardest to bite back a smile. For a woman that was known to her colleagues as stealth and light on her feet, Cliff heard her approach almost ten minutes before she made herself known. But he'd never tell her that fact. Of course, if he did, she'd most likely blame the crutches.

When he first heard her footsteps, he wasn't sure if he was elated or irritated that she had discovered his hiding spot. The path to the lake wasn't discernible to the naked eye, but now that she's here, he felt – content. As if he had been expecting her all along. And maybe he was.

When he woke this morning after the best sleep he could remember, his body had been turned toward

Alexis. She slept with a smile on her lips and Cliff prayed that he had been the one to put it there. He wanted to be the reason for all of her smiles. But just as the happy thought had planted its seed in his heart, the ugliness of who he was reared its nasty head. She didn't know him, didn't know anything about him except what the government would allow. If she ever found out about the coldness swirling through his veins, she would be disgusted.

Before morning light, he left the bed as abruptly as he had entered it, venturing outside to the place that brought him peace. Except he had forgotten his camera at his shop and felt naked standing in the open field even though he was fully clothed. The call of the water had beckoned him forward and he had been sitting in the same spot since dawn broke.

The dock had been the first thing he constructed for the property. His desire to be one with nature compelled him to take the time to sit amongst the vast space. The hard work paid off and whenever Cliff felt lost in himself, he sits in this same spot, a reminder of how inconsequential his problems were to the world.

"I was wondering where you were," she said as the thud of her crutches echoed on the wooden dock.

Cliff held out a hand and assisted Alexis in sitting on the planks, bearing most of her weight on his one hold. She giggled as she swiped her bare feet in the cool lake water, Cliff forgot that she had no shoes here, but he could listen to her laugh all day.

"Normally I come out here to clear my head," he explained.

Turning her head toward him, she prompted, "But. . ."

"But today, I'm preparing for my house to be filled to the brim with the Connelly family."

"Seems like such a burden to have people that care about you."

Her remark surprised him and he pulled his attention away from her. "I just don't like to be around a lot of people."

"Well, then you picked the wrong group of friends. I knew the day that I met them that they considered friends like family."

Cliff didn't respond. Instead, he kicked his feet gently back and forth in the water, mimicking the same moves as Alexis' feet. They stayed quiet for a few minutes, the sound of birds squawking the only noise to break their solitude.

"I. . .um. . .saw the photographs on your wall. Who took them?"

Somehow he knew that she was referring to one picture in general. The one of herself. He remembered the day he found the photograph. He had been scrolling through some candid shots of the wildlife as he normally did, but then he noticed a woman standing on the edge of the field. She had been carefree and utterly beautiful to him. After zooming in, he realized quickly that it had been the same woman he had seen jogging a few weeks before. She was looking at the wheat grains with such reverence and delicacy that he couldn't help but capture it.

"I did."

By her startled gasp, that notion seemed to surprise her.

"Really? They're beautiful, Cliff."

"Thanks. The good aim doesn't just benefit snipers, I suppose."

"Was that what you did with the Army? You were a sniper?" He knew better than to ask how she would know that information. The only thing he was confident of was that she had no clue about his current job.

"I am." He let that little token of information hang in the air, knowing that she wouldn't be satisfied with the open response.

"Do you just take pictures of nature and unassuming women?" Her voice was closer now, right near his ear and by the change in her breath, he could tell that she'd shifted closer to him.

Turning his head to face her, he's surprised at the few inches separating them. "I take pictures of things that calm me."

After her nod, Cliff waited for more questions, knowing the curious side of her was roaming freely. She surprised him again as she steered their talk in a different direction.

"Tell me about your tattoos."

His body shivered as her slender fingertips traced the dragon on his arm. Cliff had never had this kind of reaction to a woman before, not in this feral, all-consuming sense.

"They don't mean much to me personally, but they're symbolic of some things that I stand for."

"Really? Like what?" she asked as her fingertips fell to the koi fish swimming around his forearm.

"The dragon stands for strength, the koi fish for determination and good fortune, and the tiger for power."

"What about your chest?"

That was the piece he didn't want to discuss and he had been worried that she might bring it up. Grabbing her hand, halting her movements, he told her,

"That one was more complex." The thorned rose with wings was a symbol and memorial of his failed marriage.

"Oh. Well, when did you get them all? Do you want more? Oh, do you do them on yourself?" She seemed eager and genuinely intrigued as she searched his eyes for an answer, her voice perked up with each question.

"I got them after I officially left the rangers. I'm always looking to get more, but they have to stand for something. I usually call up a colleague to do my ink, I don't trust myself enough."

"That makes sense."

"I didn't notice any tattoos on you. Have any hiding?" That was what he really wanted to know. Alexis didn't seem like someone that would go get a tattoo just for the hell of it. If she had one, it definitely had a meaning to her.

He watched her skin turn from a beautiful peach flush to stark white. He began to wonder if he'd hurt her, or if she hurt herself coming out here, but he watched as her hand reached up toward her hair, tucking it behind her ear. Her hand shook the entire journey.

"Alexis?" he asked wearily, the concern for her overwhelming his senses.

She appeared like a shell of herself for a few seconds, completely lost in her own mind. Cliff worried that he's asked her something that brought back a bad memory or a terrifying moment in her life. "Alexis, I'm sorry. I didn't mean. . ."

"I had forgotten. It's not something I think about often, you know?" she whispered and Cliff ached to remove the pain he'd suddenly caused.

"I didn't mean-" he began but she quickly interrupts.

"I have a scar under my arm. I got it when I was little. That's what I tell everyone. But the truth is, my father had some of his friends hold me down and he burned a marking onto my skin. I remember the pain being unbearable. But the worst part was that my mother sat in the corner of the room watching me cry out for help." She chuckled to herself then turned to face Cliff again. "I haven't thought about that in a long time. I usually keep that information buried away with a lock and key. What was it about you that you bring out my secrets?"

Cliff swallowed but the lump in his throat made it difficult to complete the task. He couldn't believe someone would do that to a young child, would harm a single hair on her head. If he ever got his hands on her father, Cliff vowed to himself that the man would pay for his sins. Every last one of them.

"Can I. . .Can I see it?" His voice sounded strange to his own ears. He couldn't imagine what Alexis was thinking at his request.

She surprised him by lifting her shirt and raised it just under her good arm, all the way to the crease where her arm met her chest showcasing the pink scar. It was no bigger than a quarter, with eight lines crisscrossing almost resembling a three-dimensional triangle, except one of the lines continued a bit longer than the others. It was definitely a branding for the cartel, but as Cliff studies it farther, something peeks in the back of his mind. It seems familiar somehow.

Without a second thought, he reached out and traced the lines with his fingers, smiling when Alexis gasped for air at his touch. His lips begged to touch the skin, but the scar was in such an odd place that he held back. But that didn't mean when he got a chance to explore her skin fully, he wouldn't work to make it happen.

"This. . .um. . .scar was the last thing I remember about my father. Though my mother stayed silent throughout the entire process, she dropped me off at a group home the next morning.

"You know, I always wondered why my mom left me instead of packing her bags and taking us away. But now that I know what my father has been up to all these years, I'm sure she was doing what she thought was best."

"Have you thought of looking her up?" Cliff asked, brushing her hair over her shoulder.

"I did when I joined the FBI. Both she and my father disappeared without a trace. We knew where my father had been, obviously, but I wonder if he did something to my mother."

"After what we've learned, that seems like a distinct possibility. How do you feel about that?"

"I don't know. It is hard to mourn someone you haven't seen since you were seven, you know?"

Cliff understood that she wasn't waiting for a response from him as she peered out over the lake. The sun began to peek over the horizon, instantly warming the air around them. He stared at her in awe, his eyes drawn to Alexis' chestnut hair glimmering in the early morning light. She entranced him. By her strength, her wit, her beauty, Alexis was a woman that deserved far more than Cliff could give her. She deserved a gentle man that could fill her days with romance and love. Cliff's heart lost the ability to provide those things more than ten years ago.

"We should probably head inside. I'm sure Amy and her family are on their way over. Cassidy was supposed to bring you some clothes."

Cliff rose from the dock first, holding out a hand to Alexis to assist her. She struggled with the crutches, a set he had in his closet leftover from one of his missions that didn't quite go as planned. He didn't want to hamper her independence, knowing that she would rather persist through the pain, but as she struggled with every step, Cliff hold back any longer.

"Hold those crutches," he commanded as he swept her effortlessly into his arms. The fact that she didn't argue shocked him. She must have been in more pain than she let on.

Cliff continued to trek up the hill trying to find a balance between moving too fast to get her back to his house and settled in bed and moving too slow just so that he could keep her in his arms. He didn't know how long he was going to have her and he selfishly wanted to enjoy every second.

The forest blocked out the light of the sun, launching them back into the bleakness of the early morning. Alexis' hold tightened around his neck, but Cliff wasn't afraid. Not of these woods. He's walked them so many times he could find his way through them blindfolded. So many of the trees had cameras installed from his security system that he knew if something was nefariously lurking around.

"You know, I made it down here in the dark without a single worry, but now that I'm able to fully take it all in, I just want to say, I was an idiot." Cliff joined in her chuckle. He understood what she meant. Venturing out into the woods of an unknown place wasn't her smartest decision.

"Yeah, but you have good instincts. And you did find me."

"That's true."

She nuzzled closer to him, adjusting the crutches in her hold. Something was weighing her down though, he could sense it by the way she wouldn't make eye contact with him.

"Cliff?" There it was.

He could feel her stare pinned to the side of his face, but he made no move to turn his attention toward her.

"Yeah?"

"I have a question about one of the photos. The one on your mantle," she began and Cliff's heart began to seize. Sweat gathered along the back of his neck, right at the hairline. If he were carrying anyone else, he would drop them on their ass, pack up his things, and move to a new town to start over again. But he couldn't do that to Alexis when she needed him most. "Who is the woman in the photograph?"

She sensed his uneasiness at the question and tried to backpedal, stuttering an apology, but the wound has been freshly opened. They stepped through the edge of the woods, the cabin in view, and from across the field, Cliff could make out a caravan of cars and trucks heading their way. Their time of solitude was about to be broken. But her question weighed heavily on him. Cliff was alarmed at his desire to share this secret with her, to share a piece of himself that she wouldn't find in any of his files, he had removed them himself on purpose.

The words tumble forward, surprising him. "That woman was my wife."

Her grip around his neck tightened and he wished he was able to read her thoughts, but as Cliff took a second to peer down at her, he could read it clearly on her face. She was so expressive. A mixture of anger, confusion, and joy all gaped up at him through her eyes. They were wide like a child's. Her lips parted with her slackened jaw, but it was the slight tilt at the corner of her mouth that had him explaining more.

"Being a military wife wasn't easy, and Stacy couldn't handle me being gone for so long. She began abusing prescription medications thinking that she could keep it hidden. It wasn't something like heroin or cocaine, but opioids are just as powerful."

"What happened?" Alexis whimpered against his neck.

"She wanted her next fix more than she wanted her next breath, and she was willing to do anything and everything to get it. The police were never able to determine if it was murder or suicide. It happened when I was on my first tour."

"Oh, Cliff. You both were so young," she cried as they reentered the cabin through the back door. He didn't want to hear her pity; he'd heard enough of it since Stacy's death, which was why only a few in Carson knew that he was previously married at all. The blame and guilt of her death still weighed heavily on his shoulders. "I'm so sorry for what you've gone through."

In the bedroom, Cliff settled her back on the mattress, but as he began to pull away, she settled her good hand on the side of his face. "Thank you for sharing that with me."

Cliff reached up and clapped her wrist in his hold, letting it linger, unsure if he wanted to keep her hand on his face or pull it away. The strength in her touch was addictive, his own personal drug. He wondered if this was what Stacy had been fixated on.

His gaze swept across her face, cataloging her features to memory.

Their bodies were so close, too close. If Cliff moved just a few inches, he could bring their lips together, taking the taste he'd been dreaming of for years. But as he contemplated his next move, Alexis made it for him. She leaned forward and in one swift motion, sealed their lips together. His spark of awareness ignited immediately and he had to mentally refrain himself from gripping her in his arms and tossing her across the bed to have his nefarious way with her. Instead, he rooted himself to the floor allowing Alexis the chance to explore his mouth. He opened up to her willingly as her tongue licked at his lips. She tasted like heaven and mint and Cliff realized she found the spare toothbrush he had left her in the bathroom this morning.

A knock on his front door sounded causing them to pull apart at the interruption, Alexis groaned at their loss of contact.

"I'll go let them in. You can take your time joining us."

Rose painted her cheeks and Cliff grinned at her reaction to their kiss, something he wanted to repeat soon.

Lifting her chin with his finger, he waited for her eyes to meet his. "We'll do that again once everyone leaves."

Playfully Alexis replied, "Promise?"

"The entire town couldn't keep me away."

Hating every step as he moved away, Cliff reached into his dresser, pulled out a T-shirt and quickly covered his chest. He did the same with a pair of camouflage shorts, removing his gym shorts in the process.

"I'll bring back Cassidy's clothes when she arrives."

"Oh, that would be great. I can't believe I get to wear one of her designs," Alexis said with elation. If she were able, Cliff guessed that she would clap her hands together while bouncing up and down on the bed. Her excitement was palpable. He may be a military man, but even he knew that Cassidy was the world's most sought after designer.

As he stepped toward the door at the sound of another knock, Alexis reached her hand out and clutched his arm, wanting his attention.

"Cliff. Thank you. . .for sharing that with me."

He knew that she referred to the story about his wife, but he didn't want to let the feelings of hurt and betrayal ruin their intimate moment.

Gazing down at her Cliff said, "Don't worry, we'll share some more kisses later." He winked as she released her hold on him and headed out of the bedroom hoping that his visitors were enough of a distraction to keep his thoughts far away from their kiss. Otherwise, he'd be too busy counting down the seconds until he can do it again.

***

Voices filtered into the room and Alexis tried to count them. Four at first, but continuously growing. She couldn't pinpoint which one belonged to whom and that left her nerves in shambles.

After her night of sleep, Alexis felt considerably better. The ache in her shoulder remained, but it was not as sharp as before. Now, it was more of a dull ache, the same with her leg. Even as a kid Alexis had been a quick healer. She remembered Logan advised her to keep weight off of her left for a few days, but he should know that she was not one to follow directions.

As she waited for a set of clean clothes to dress in, Alexis thought back to what she just learned about Cliff. A widower wasn't the first thing that would have come to her mind when describing him, but now that she knew, she could see that it made up a big part of who he was. She couldn't imagine losing someone you loved when you were thousands of miles away. It was no wonder he kept himself closed off from others. But why had he agreed to help protect her? That was another point she needed to bring up with him. Alexis was afraid that the longer she spent in this town with him, the stronger her feelings for him may become, and that could only put them both in danger. And if her father got wind of Cliff in her life, a bullseye would be painted in bright red on his back.

But her father and his group were coming for her anyway. When? She had zero doubts that he was biding his time. Someone that was able to take himself off the map and radar of the FBI, DEA, and probably every other government agency in existence was used to taking his time to get what he wanted. What Alexis couldn't figure out was what her role was in all of this. Maybe the conversation today could help answer that.

Feeling like a lifetime has passed, Cliff strolled back into the room, bags upon bags of clothes dangling from his arms. God, he was gorgeous. Even dressed down he had a powerful air about him. And that damn T-shirt looked like it wanted to rip itself in half just to give the world another glimpse of his perfect chest. She was one lucky girl.

"I think she brought you her entire store," he joked as he sets the bags on the bed.

Alexis leaned over and started rummaging through the contents. A red dress caught her eye and she held it up, eyebrow cocked in question.

"How long does she think I'm staying? A year?"

"It's hard to say. Maybe Cassidy just wanted to make sure that you had options."

Giggling, Alexis pointed out, "Where in Carson would I ever need to wear a dress like this?"

She watched in awe as he delicately slipped the material from her hands and glided his thumb back and forth across the dress. "Maybe not in Carson, but there are some beautiful restaurants and wineries close by."

"Oh," she mumbled, watching him in reverence as he gently placed the dress back on the bed. "Um, did she happen to pack any undergarments? Otherwise, I may need to take a trip to the local department store."

Cliff's throat bobbed and Alexis couldn't help but smile knowing that she caught him off guard with her question. She didn't care if she wore plain cotton or supple silks, Alexis had always loved lingerie. Being in the FBI didn't leave her many options in that department when she was on the field. Sweat and silk didn't go very well together.

Silk sheets on the other hand, was something she could get behind. Or on top of. An image of her and Cliff rolling around on his bed came to mind and she found herself blushing, the heat rising on her cheeks and flaming her skin. Alexis ducked her head out of his view, but she was too slow. His grin widened as he crouched down to her eye level.

"Tell me what you were thinking just now."

Alexis raised her head in defiance. "I wasn't thinking about anything."

"Yes, you were."

Schooling her features, Alexis hoped that Cliff dropped the subject, but he met her stare head-on.

They played a mental game of cat versus mouse, and though Alexis was usually triumphant against her colleagues, she found herself melting into Cliff's stare with each passing second.

With a grunt she relented control, "Fine, I was just thinking of silk sheets, if you must know."

Reaching out, he fingered the edge of her shirt, sliding his hand back and forth. Alexis sucked in a breath as the back of his fingers caressed the soft skin of her stomach. She involuntarily sucked in her waist.

"What kinds of things with sheets? Did you imagine lying naked on top of them? Maybe with a man pressing you down against the silk?"

"Um. . ." she replied, licking her lips. His eyes followed the movement of her tongue as it peeked out.

"Did you imagine *me* pressing you against the silk sheets, Alexis?" he asked, his voice huskier than before. The sound had her body quaking under his touch.

"Um. . ." she repeated, wholly lost in a fog of his making.

"That's what I thought." Straightening his stance, Alexis instantly felt the air cool around her. "Think about how it would be in real life instead of a daydream. Need any help getting dressed or could you manage?"

"I. . ." she started, then had to clear her throat to continue. "I think I can manage. Thanks."

"Okay, I'll see you out there."

Cliff closed the door with a soft click and Alexis sifted through the clothes again, settling on some undergarments she found, a blue sundress, and a pair of flat brown sandals. The dress she'd chosen had buttons going down the front and she assumed that it would make it easier to put on. Disappointment flourished as it took her a few extra minutes to maneuver the material around her hands to get the button through the loop. By the time she got all thirty of the buttons secure, Alexis began to feel a bit light-headed. She hadn't grabbed anything to eat before she went on her journey to find Cliff this morning and she could only hope that he had something she could snack on in front of his friends without looking like a pig. In the back of her mind, she recalled Amy's visit the night before and the mention of food.

Alexis took one look in the mirror and scrutinized herself. Bruises marred her skin, scratches and cuts ran up and down her arms and legs. She was quite a sight. Running her good hand along her neck, she realized that her locket was missing. The only piece she had to remember her family. Alexis swore that she had it on when Heath had shoved her into the back of the vehicle two days ago.

Knowing this was as good as she was going to look, Alexis secured the arm brace in place, opened the bedroom door, and stepped into the hallway. Immediately her sense of smell filled with the aroma of pancakes. A loud grumble sounded from her stomach and she couldn't fight against the laugh.

Moving farther down the hall, Alexis hoped to sneak her way into the kitchen unnoticed and help herself to that wonderful scent, but just as she turned the corner, she bumped into Cassidy.

"Oh, excuse me. I'm sorry," Alexis mumbled as she braced an arm against the wall.

"That was completely my fault. It's good to see you, Alexis, though not under these circumstances." Cassidy's eyes trailed up and down Alexis' body, clapping her hands during the process. "I see you found something to wear. That is one of my favorite dresses. It's part of my summer line."

All the blood drained from Alexis' face. She assumed that these clothes were from the clearance rack or from several seasons ago. Alexis never expected to receive something so current. This dress cost more than the apartment she rented.

"Don't you dare try to give me back those clothes either," the business shark before her argued. "You're the perfect sample size. The only difference is that you have lean muscle on your frame. You wear the dress beautifully. Now, I do believe we have a few people waiting for you, and a certain man that we're driving a bit stir crazy."

Cassidy gripped Alexis' free arm with unexpected strength. Together they ventured into the living room, Alexis held her breath the entire time. She hadn't seen these people in over two years and she was worried about how they would react at her bringing danger their way.

The chatter in the living room quieted the moment she trailed behind Cassidy into the room.

She wasn't sure how to react. If she should smile, cringe, run and hide. At the moment, all of those seemed like a better plan than the blank, deer in the headlights look she was sure showed on her face.

"Um. . .hello everyone," she murmured with a vulnerability Alexis hadn't felt in years.

In unison, the group began speaking all at once. Some tossing questions her way, others offering their sympathies, it was almost a bit too much for Alexis to handle. She'd been on her fair share of interrogations, mostly on the delivery end. This was the first time she'd been the one receiving.

Her head swung back and forth, not sure who to respond to first, confident she was going to get whiplash at the speed she moved from question to question.

A gentle hand landed on her lower back offering Alexis a solace she didn't realize that she needed. Since walking into the room, she caught her breath for the first time. The relief was instantaneous and welcoming.

"Let's get you some food, okay? Their questions can wait."

"That sounds good. Thank you."

Cliff guided her toward a small table fit for two that she hadn't noticed this morning during her exploration.

"I thought I smelled pancakes," she mentioned as the group started chatting amongst themselves again.

"You would be correct," Cliff said as he strutted toward the kitchen, quickly returning with a stack of fluffy pancakes.

"Wow, I'm not sure I can eat all of this." Alexis' eyes widened at the amount of carb-filled goodness laid before her.

"Take it slow. You don't have much in your stomach and I don't want you to overdo it." Cliff sat across from her, his weighted stare penetrating through every ounce of her skin.

Alexis only made it through a quarter of the stack, the three pancakes settling her hunger. Cliff cleaned her mess despite her arguments to do it herself. She wasn't used to being waited on hand and foot, but she couldn't deny that she could get used to it.

Cliff loomed over her at the table, his deep brown eyes roaming over her body. He was, by far, the most attractive man that she ever met. A few strands of his dark brown hair fell over his eyes and Alexis lifted her hand to swipe it back into place. She gasped at the contact as the back of her finger touched his forehead. Their eyes locked and the sounds in the next room fell away. It was just the two of them.

But Alexis wondered if she and Cliff were attracted by convenience. Would things be different for them if she wasn't being chased by the cartel and needed his help?

Cliff reached up and gripped her wrist, tugging her hand close to his mouth. He pressed a gentle kiss on the palm of her hand and Alexis' lips parted, wishing that his lips were settling against hers.

"Sorry we're late, guys," a delicate voice called out from the front door, adding to the large gathering. "We needed to drop the kids off with Poppy," the new guest added, mentioning the Connelly's youngest son's wife.

"Now that Logan and Avery are here, we can't keep them waiting much longer," Cliff pointed out, breaking their moment.

The mood of the room shifted as Cliff pulled Alexis into the room, Mama Connelly moved from her seat on the couch and offered it to Alexis. Though she didn't know many of the group that well, it warmed her heart to see Amy perch herself on the knee of her husband, Joseph. They were all there for her, to help protect her and catch her father.

She still struggled to come to terms with the fact that her father was the man she and her team has been tracking for years. The man that used to sing her lullabies as a baby and taught her how to tie her shoes before starting kindergarten.

"So," Dylan addressed the group and they collectively turned their attention to him. "I'm sure by now you all know the gist of what happened and why Alexis is here. Because the mission is ongoing, I can't divulge the background. But I will let Alexis tell you what she knows, and then we'll devise a plan to keep her safe. But make no mistake, these men are notorious for tying up loose ends, they will come to find her. The question is when."

Squaring her shoulders, Alexis adjusted herself in the seat, sitting straighter than a moment ago. But what gave her strength was the feeling of Cliff's hands resting on her shoulders.

"Thanks, everyone, for dealing with all of this trouble I've caused," Alexis began, then delved into what happened during the mission. She explained how she had to outrun some of the cartel's henchmen, getting shot in the process. Had it not been for Heath, she would have died out in the field.

"How did you know that it was your father? Could you possibly have confused him with someone that merely resembled him? It seems like it has been a while since you have seen him."

Instinctively Alexis reached toward her neck, mindlessly trying to grasp her locket which was missing.

"My locket," she murmured, turning her attention toward Logan and Dylan, both leaning against the wall. "Did you find my locket when I arrived? It is um. . .important to me."

Reaching into his pocket Logan stepped toward the couch, clasping the thin gold chain and heart in his hand."

"I found it on the ground outside of Cliff's shop. I assumed it was yours, so I held onto it."

The heart dangled in front of Alexis' face swinging back and forth like a pendulum. With a shaking hand, she clasped the delicate piece and held it close.

"Thank you," she told him, unable to meet his eyes.

"How are you feeling?" Logan whispered.

"Good, tired."

"As expected. If it is okay with you, I'd like to check the wounds before we leave."

Before she had a chance to answer, Alexis felt Cliff's hold on her good shoulder tighten in a supportive squeeze.

"Yeah, um. . .that would be fine."

Logan nodded and moved back beside his wife then wrapped a protective arm around her waist. Alexis' heart squeezed in her chest as she watched their exchange. It was not something she ever saw for herself, always thinking that she wasn't good enough for that kind of love and affection. If her parents were so willing to toss her aside, how could she imagine that a man wouldn't do the same? Though she had known Cliff for two years, it was always at a distance. Now that they seem to share a mutual attraction, she was afraid that he was still too closed off to pursue a relationship.

Not that she was in the right frame of mind to begin anything with anyone. Despite the cartel coming after her, she hadn't been intimate with anyone since college. The FBI made sure that her life revolved around them and them alone.

Joseph, the patriarch of the Connelly family, leaned forward with his elbows resting on his knees. His knowing eyes pinned to her, but regardless of the sense of authority permeating from him, his gaze reflected a sheer kindness in them.

To her, Joseph was the perfect father figure. She knew that he had fathered Avery while he and Amy had been separated, but that didn't change her opinion of him. If anything, it strengthened it. Not many men were willing to acknowledge and accept their mistake.

"Can you tell us why this locket seems so important to you?" he asked. Anyone else that would have asked that question would have had Alexis on defense, but not Joseph. He was inquisitive about why she's white-knuckling the jewelry.

"Oh, it was the last thing I have from my parents before they sent me away. It's the only piece left of them." Joseph and the rest of the group nodded in understanding, but their eyes widened as she further explained, "It is also how I know that the man I saw was my father."

Using her chipped thumbnail, Alexis opened the locket in half, a smile immediately spreading across her lips as she stared down at a miniature picture of her mother and father. Regardless of them giving her up, she still loved them. Which made the knowledge of her father's hobby difficult to fathom.

Alexis held up the locket for the room to see, pointing out the image of her father. Besides gray patches around his temples, he looked exactly the same as he had in the portrait.

She extended her hand, letting the chain and locket dangle from her fingers.

"The man I saw in the bunker is the same man in this picture."

Dylan was the first to move closer, narrowing his gaze as he took in the man's image.

"Shit," he bellowed as he quickly moved out of the room and down the hall with his phone pressed to his ear. The others in the room all leaned in and looked at the tiny picture.

"If it is okay with you, Alexis, I'd like to make a copy of the picture and share it with the residents in town so that we can have everyone on alert," Joseph said.

"Okay, that seems like a good idea."

"We need to get Preston involved too. The police need to be notified so they can monitor the town and surrounding counties."

Collectively the group agreed and for the first time, Alexis breathed a sigh of relief. These people really were going to help her. She had thought it was a silly notion at first, but now she could see that they would do anything to keep her safe.

From behind her, a voice bellowed, the sound dark and deep in its command. "Hand me the locket." Alexis wanted to object, never one to be told what to do. She and authority never meshed well together. How she had been able to last so long in the FBI, she would never know.

As she turned in her seat, her gaze met the angry stare of Cliff's. But as her eyes flicked back and forth, she could see that he was looking at the necklace, not at her.

She placed the heart in his hand and dropped the thin chain from her fingers. Around her, the group quieted as Cliff inspected the piece. His shrewd eyes took in every detail.

"You've had this a while?" he asked as he brought the small trinket closer to his eyes.

"Yes."

"And it has always been with you?"

"Well, yes. I never take it off, and it must have fallen off outside your shop considering the circumstances."

Cliff nodded and turned to step out of the room, his heavy stomps leading toward his kitchen. Confusion blossomed as she stared at his retreating back, even through his tight T-shirt she could see his muscles hunched around his shoulders.

Something nagged at the back of her mind, some other occasion that she went without the necklace. As a child in a group home, she learned quickly that if you wanted to keep any of your personal belongings, you kept them on your person at all times. Then you reduced the risk of another child stealing or breaking them. Or worse, the adult taking it and sometimes selling the item. Alexis saw so many beautiful heirlooms taken from the younger ones and pawned for a quick buck.

Finally, a memory popped into her mind and Alexis found herself jumping from her seat, as fast as someone injured could.

"Cliff!" she called out as she hobbled back toward the hallway, only to collide with a broad chest as she made it around the couch without her crutches. She had been using every available surface to keep herself balanced.

"I remember something. For my high school graduation, the guardian of the group home I was in took the locket to get it cleaned for me. She was one of the nicer ones and I trusted her."

Nodding at her recollection, Cliff glided his hand down her arm until he clasped Alexis' hand.

Tugging it toward him, he flipped it over, her palm faced upward toward the ceiling.

"You shouldn't have," he explained and she gasped in horror as he placed her locket on her palm with the back removed. A small black object attached to the inside of the backing caught her eye.

"What's th-" she began, but Cliff continued. "My guess is your father had been tracking you. In the group home and because of social services he could always keep an eye on where you were, even manipulating your location if he wanted. When you graduated high school, which is a rarity in the system, I might add, he knew if he wanted to continue knowing where you were at all times, then he had to do something drastic.

"I'm sure it didn't take much convincing to get his hands on the necklace and place the tracking system inside. It's one I've seen before, very popular in the late nineteen nineties."

What little strength Alexis possessed at the moment immediately dissipates into the air. Her shoulders drooped toward the floor as she hung her head. Betrayal – that's what she felt. Complete and utter betrayal.

"So, he's always known where I've been?"

Cliff's hand pressed onto her shoulder, his attention doing little to brighten her mood.

"Yes, which means he knew you were arriving at his bunker," Cliff seethed, his voice sounding pained to Alexis' ears. She pulled her gaze from the jewelry resting on her palm to the man standing before her.

"That explains why the women were moved."

"It also means that he set you up and knowingly had his men shoot at you. I'm not sure what he's up to because he's had ample time to take you out since you've been here."

Her face blanched, all warmth drained from her skin as she took in his words. Her father was truly a heartless bastard. It almost made her sick to her stomach knowing that she was related to him, that they shared DNA.

"I think I'm going to be sick," she explained, her gut churning.

"That's not the worst of our problems. I need to run it through my scanner, but if your father is who I think he is – we're going to have more than just a few men on our tails."

From behind her, a voice called out from the hallway, "What do we need to do?" She recognized it as Dylan.

"We need to take this thing as far away as possible."

She really hoped that he was referring to the necklace, because for the first time, Alexis was tired of running. For once, she wanted to stay.

Chapter Five

C liff hated that he had to leave Alexis just after she learned that her father had been tracking her for all these years. He knew that she was strong, but she still mourned the loss of her family, and knowing that her father had ample opportunities to reconnect was a bit more than he thought Alexis could handle right now. Not three or four days ago, she watched her entire team get shot down and killed at the hand of her father.

"So, explain to me again what we're doing," Preston asked.

Cliff turned away from looking out the passenger window and focused on the town sheriff, Preston. He didn't know much about the man except what was in his file, but Cliff was impressed when he learned of the man's years of undercover work. Cliff also knew that Preston had deceived and lied to Sydney and Dylan at one point. The sheriff was still working to get in the Connelly's good graces.

"We need to make it look like Alexis skipped town. Bide ourselves more time before her father descends onto Carson. And he would come here looking for her."

"And you thought a five-hour trip one way to Raleigh was a good idea?"

"Yes. There is a major airport and it is big enough that it will appear that Alexis is trying to hide out with a larger crowd. I found an abandoned warehouse; we can take the locket before I place it in my transmission blocker."

When Cliff had remembered the heavy black box in his closet, elation had spiraled through him. After finding the tracking system in Alexis' locket, the gathering in his living room had instantly grown quiet. The room was filled with fear and anger. But he was glad he was able to put some of them at ease. It only took a few minutes for him and Dylan to concoct a plan to deter the cartel chasing after Alexis. He was surprised when Alexis agreed to stay with Dylan while Cliff went off to complete the task.

"And you needed me to use my authority to get us there faster," Preston clarified.

"Bingo."

Leaning toward the driver's side, Cliff smiled as he read the speedometer at almost one hundred miles per hour. He had drowned out the sounds of the sirens nearly two hours into their trip.

The GPS guided them to their destination, and together, the men carried the locket toward an upper floor of the abandoned warehouse, appearing to be inhabited by the homeless at some point recently based on the urine smell permeating in the space.

As they traveled back toward Carson, the necklace now safe in the blocking box, Cliff texted Dylan to meet him at his studio office. After prying the picture of her parents from the inside of the locket, Cliff wanted to run them through his government-issued scanner to see if it picked up on anyone.

He also wanted to rest his eyes on the woman he's sworn to protect. He could only assume that she was feeling a bit lost and confused at what she learned this morning. So, when he arrived at his studio, Preston followed him out of the car. Cliff was surprised to find a determined Alexis sitting on his steps with Dylan.

The corner of his lips tilted upward in a smirk. He should have known that she would want to be a part of figuring out what they're up against and devising a plan.

Wordlessly he bent down and lifted her into his arms, being mindful of the dress she wore, and carried her up the steps. Alexis buried her head against his shoulder and Cliff released a deep sigh that had been bottled up since this morning. He wanted nothing more than to place his lips against hers, strip her bare, and finally feel her wrapped around him. But as he set her on her feet as they reached the landing at the top of the stairs, he settled for a quick peck against her mouth.

Cliff waited for the other men to reach the landing, placed his finger in a biometric scanner, leaned close to a small blue light that scanned his retina before twisting the knob to unlock the door.

"This goes without saying, but none of you know that this exists. Okay?" he explained to everyone, but his gaze was pointed toward Preston's.

Cliff didn't wait for a response as he ushered everyone inside the shop's upstairs apartment.

"Wow, this is quite the setup," Preston murmured as Cliff watched him take in the large monitors hanging on the walls and the six computers set up beneath them. Cliff couldn't help but think that this wasn't anything compared to the quadruple locked bedroom down the hall that kept computers allowing him access to every government agency and their files. Hell, even he was impressed with that room and all of its gadgets.

Dylan assisted Alexis into a chair facing the central computer while Cliff took the seat closest to him.

Underneath her breath, Cliff could hear Alexis grumble, "Reconnaissance team my ass." He chuckled at her observation. Cliff knew that it wouldn't take her long to figure out that he did so much more for his government than scout locations and information. He was surprised that Dylan hadn't figured it out yet, or maybe he had and just kept his mouth shut. After all, Dylan still worked with the FBI on a secret team that Cliff wasn't sure that his wife Sydney was aware of.

"Okay, let's see if we can identify your family in our files then see how much time we have."

"Time we have for what?" Preston asked.

Cliff let Preston's question linger in the air as he pulled out a small scanner. Lifting the plastic bag containing her father and mother's pictures inside, he rested the images on the glass.

From beside him, he watched Alexis' eyes widen as the screen displayed thousands of images per second, a red square narrowed in on the similar physical characteristics of the pictures.

"I bet Jameson would love to get his hands on this program," Preston added, leaning forward to watch the screen as well. Jameson was the software genius of the Connelly family.

Cliff couldn't bite back his chuckle. "Who do you think was commissioned to create it?"

Suddenly the images began to slow down and the red light of the scanner dimmed, alerting Cliff that the application was almost complete. He pulled the plastic bag away from the device and gently returned it to Alexis who barely noticed through her stare at the screen.

A red X marred the image of her mother with the title unidentifiable typed below. Alexis gasped as she read the information and Cliff wanted nothing more than to ease her pain.

"Hey, it just means there was no criminal activity on her so she couldn't be identified."

"Or. . ." she pushed as she turned to look at him, questions in her distressed gaze.

"Or nothing. If you can remember your mother's full and maiden name, we can run a search in another application after we identify your father. I'm certain he won't be using your family name."

Pings sound on the computer, drawing Alexis' attention back to the screen. Cliff continued to look at her for a moment, wishing he had the right to scoop her up and take her away from everything. He had the means to go off the grid to a remote location, and he would if he had even the slightest of inklings that she would join him willingly. For now, he could only protect her here in Carson.

He studied her face for a second more, memorizing the lines around her mouth and eyes – laugh lines Mrs. Connelly called them, but right now, the corners of her mouth are turned down into a scowl. Alexis was too beautiful for that expression.

Pulling his attention away, Cliff glanced at the monitor where a picture and a name shone brightly. As Alexis had explained, the wanted poster looked almost identical to the one from her locket, only more graying in the hair. The man had barely aged.

"Lev Dison," she reads aloud.

Shaking his head, Cliff clarified the name, "Devil Son. It was sort of like an anagram for the name he's known for by the government. He's been captured twice. Once, for drug trafficking, which he got out of. Second, for solicitation of a minor almost eight years ago. My guess is that was the start of the sex trafficking. He's been unseen for years."

"Until now," Dylan added in.

"Okay, so what information did this give us?" Alexis asked more calmly than Cliff was expecting.

Nodding, Cliff moved the mouse to click on the image, bringing up hundreds of known cartel members and associated criminals. "What it means, especially with the newest technologies in big cities to counter terrorist activity, we can monitor any movement from these known links."

Scrolling down the screen, Cliff commited to memory the faces and names listed. But at the end, Cliff found himself jerking back in his seat as if the computer mouse had burned his hand.

"Dude, what is it?" Dylan asked as Alexis simultaneously questioned.

Cliff couldn't answer, unable to form the right words, but launched himself out of the chair, leaving it spinning in his wake. Glancing over his shoulder, Cliff watched as Dylan leaned closer toward the screen, reading the name on the list. His friend's back straightened in alarm as the information sank in.

"No. No fucking way."

"What? What is it?" Alexis' startled voice rang around the room as Cliff hauled her out of her chair, lifting her arm in the process.

He knew that the scar looked familiar, but now that he had more information on her father, he knew precisely why he'd branded his daughter. It wasn't for a family marking as she had assumed. No, her father burned her skin for future payment. He planned to use her if he was ever in deep shit.

"Fuck, fuck, fuck," Cliff repeated as he held her arm in the air, her pink scarring visible just over the stitching of her dress. "Dylan, look." As his friend moved to get a closer look, Cliff explained, "It is her symbol, just upside down."

"Harposia," they say in unison.

"Son of a bitch, that demonic woman tried to kill my wife." Dylan's hands thrusted through his short hair.

"Harposia?" Alexis inquired. "The same Harposia I helped move into a maximum-security prison?"

"One in the same," Cliff said through gritted teeth as he relaxed her arm back down at her side. Harposia was known in many criminal circles. With the face of a grandmother, that woman could bring world leaders to their knees. And she had, numerous times. There was no telling how many small countries and rulers gain their weapons and drugs from her businesses. She was a nasty woman that always got what she wanted.

"And you think my father works with her? There is no way. We infiltrated her entire system," Alexis explained, the octaves of her voice rising in panic.

"Leaders like Harposia never show all of their cards. They have their fingers in multiple side groups with multiple upper management. You have to think of her as the head of a major international corporation; even if you dismantle one branch the rest will still flourish. Someone like Harposia will have her business running for decades," Dylan explained, his words clipped and filled with anger.

Alexis curled her good arm across her chest, almost as if shielding herself. "So, what you're saying is, that I'll never be safe. Someone somewhere will always have a hit out on my head."

The growl came quickly, reverberating from deep in his chest as he bellowed, "No."

Alexis pinned him with a stare he'd never seen from her before and if he were in any other situation, he might get a bit turned on by her dominance.

Unfortunately, he was too unsettled to take pleasure in her change of mood.

"I don't think you get a say in this," she stated.

Cliff approached her until he stood only a few inches away, the top of her head grazing his chin, causing her to look up at him. "I get every say in this. I agreed to protect you and I will do so with my life. Do you understand?" he harshly whispered, each word enunciated as if it would be his last.

The worry about the bounty on Alexis sent shivers down his spine. Her father was using her to make a statement and proving to Harposia that he could tie up loose ends. And by selling her to the highest bidder, he's ensuring that he got money as well.

And if Cliff failed her, his life wouldn't be worth living.

Their eyes pinned each other in place, each one waiting for the other to break their stare, but this was a game Cliff was all too familiar with. The technique of intimidation weighed in his favor.

A cough sounded from behind them and they pulled their gazes away. "Not to intrude, but I need to go get in touch with the local FBI branch and let them know what's going on," Dylan began, but Cliff immediately shot him down. "No. We don't want there to be any knowledge of Alexis being here. None. There is no doubt a mole somewhere working under

Harposia's payroll. She's powerful, Dylan, you know this. Reach out to Heath and let him get some intel under the radar. He can play it off as an investigation on his team's mission."

"And what do you suggest we do in the meantime? Wait like sitting ducks?"

"Absolutely not. We make sure Lev's picture is seen by everyone in the town. We use the town chat and the Lady Busy Bees to our advantage to share information. You know that nothing in this town was kept quiet.

"Lev could strike one day from now, or one month, there isn't much information on his MO, but we know he's going to want to get rid of the situation sooner rather than later, especially if he is afraid of word getting back to Harposia. She may be in jail, but she is certainly fed information."

Chiming in, Alexis asked, "And what am I going to do?"

Smirking at the feisty woman, Cliff said, "You're going to rest up and get ready for the biggest fight of your life."

***

God, it was so hot, Alexis thought to herself as she rolled over again, wincing as she put too much pressure on her shoulder. Logan had said earlier that she was healing well, and after a few more days and some shoulder exercises, she would be back to normal. She had almost kissed the man; she was so thankful. Alexis had been more than ready to get a gun in her hand and target practice. It was her favorite way to relieve stress, and after everything she learned that evening, she needed to get her head on straight sooner rather than later.

Flipping around to rest on her back again, Alexis huffed as she stared up at the ceiling. Even in the mountains of North Carolina, it could be sweltering at night. Cliff explained that he had central air installed in the cabin, but as a precaution wanted to leave it turned off so that he could hear better. Alexis understood, she really did, but damn it was so freaking hot she was certain she had soaked through the mattress.

An idea formulated in the back of her mind, a dip in the lake would be a dream in this heat. She wondered if she could get Cliff to join her; even in the darkness Alexis was sure she'd be able to make out every hard muscle of his body.

Alexis tossed her legs off the bed, the rest of her body following suit, and she tugged at the soaked oversized T-shirt clinging to her heated skin. She flexed her toes against the cool floor, savoring the relief on the bottom of her feet. She was half tempted to lay her entire body on the old hardwood.

Opening the bedroom door, another wave of heat from the narrow hallway assaulted her, but as she made her way into the living room, the air cooled significantly. It was refreshing as the cross breeze from the open front and back windows glided across her skin.

"Hey, what are you doing awake?" Cliff asked, his gaze pulled away from the laptop. She wondered if he ever slept. "Thinking about your mom?"

She had been. After Dylan and Preston left the apartment, she and Cliff launched another software application that came up empty on searching her mother's name. Cliff assured her that he would reach out to his contacts to see if they could learn anything more, but her fractured heart broke by the minute.

She didn't want to lie to Cliff, but she also didn't want to discuss her parents anymore, so she settled by telling him that she was too hot.

"You're welcome to rest out here if it is cooler. I can take the bedroom."

God, this man was a saint. Since she arrived, he'd been bending over backward for her. And what had she done for him? Not a damn thing.

"Actually, think I could just hang out here with you for a while? I'm not very tired."

Cliff closed his laptop, basking the room in darkness. "Met your quota for sleep?" he joked as the television across from him came to life. He immediately turned down the volume.

"Something like that," she giggled as she moved to sit beside him on the couch, a good foot away from each other.

"So, tell me, Alexis, what's something about you I won't find in your government file."

"Is this how we get to know each other?"

"Something like that." He repeated her words and she turned to look at him, both of them smiling widely. Even with the bluish tone from the television casting light on their faces, she could see how tense he was. Alexis wished that she could witness him relaxed, carefree.

"Something not in my file," she mused, moving her glance toward the ceiling. "Um, when I was little, I thought I'd become a veterinarian. I loved animals. Still do. What about you?"

"I tried to keep tabs on you since you left Carson two years ago. Lost track about a year later."

Her mouth hung agape at his confession. She never would have expected that he would have monitored her. Any other time Alexis would feel violated, but right now, she felt a sense of elation.

"I looked you up after the first time Dylan teamed us up together. There wasn't much in your file, as you know, but I was curious none-the-less."

In a movement so quick, Alexis found herself straddling Cliff's lap. Their faces were only an inch or two apart and the growing hardness between his legs pressed against her smoldering center.

One of Cliff's strong hands dove into her hair, clenching the strands as he tugged her face closer.

"Why did you look me up?"

Softly Cliff replied, "I wanted to make sure that you were real," before he smashed their mouths together, his strong hold controlled every tilt of her head and twist of her neck.

He possessed her, fully and completely. And as his tongue peeked out, seeking entrance, she willingly obliged, loving the way he explored her mouth. On their own, her hips began to rock against him, searching for the hard friction of his erection. A moan escaped her lips as his other hand trailed up her thigh, his thumb moving toward her panties.

Cliff pulled his lips away from her mouth and began leaving a path of kisses from her jawline and down her neck.

"My real name isn't Cliff," he mumbled against her skin and Alexis made a mental note to ask for more information on that tidbit later.

In one quick swoop, he lifted the shirt off her body, leaving her bare except for a pair of pale pink cotton panties.

"God, you're fucking gorgeous," he groaned before leaning forward and capturing one of her nipples in his mouth. "And sweet," he added as he moved toward her other breast. The wetness cooling her heated skin.

"Cliff, please," she cried out, her hips rocking against him as his hand tried to hold her still.

"What is it you want, Alexis?" Cliff peppered kisses along the tops of her breasts, his tongue sweeping out as he reached the valley between them.

"I want you, your lips, your tongue, your cock, all of it." Her voice sounded breathy to her own ears and so unfamiliar. She had no time to wonder what siren had taken over her body as Cliff slipped his hand down the front of her panties. The second the pad of his finger brushed against her clit, she jerked in his arms, the sensation both foreign and welcome.

Pressing his lips against her mouth, he murmured, "You're so fucking wet and hot. I can't wait to slip my dick inside you."

Alexis didn't realize that she could orgasm from words alone, but as Cliff's voice skirted across her skin as he deftly rubbed circles around her clit, she quickly felt the tension growing in her abdomen.

"Cliff, please," she begged, swaying her hips back and forth, crying out as he slipped his finger deep in her channel.

"This what you want, sweet girl?" he asked as his lips pressed kisses repeatedly along her jawline.

Alexis felt the pull as he fucked her gently with his fingers, using his palm to rub against her sensitive nerves. Only a few seconds passed until she shattered at his hand, a smile etched on her lips. She missed this. Missed being intimate with a man. Missed being taken care of. Missed taking care of someone.

Her breath came in heavy pants as she opened her eyes to find Cliff's lustful gaze pinned to hers. His chest moved up and down, not in exertion, but in need. He was holding himself back. And that was absolutely what she didn't want.

Leaning forward, she sealed her lips against his, sucking his bottom lip into her mouth, nibbling on the soft skin. Her hand reached down and slid beneath the waistband of his gym shorts, wrapping around his hard cock. She couldn't see it, but by touch, she could tell that he was beyond the size of the average man. But Alexis expected nothing less. She got satisfaction at the way Cliff jerked against her palm.

She ran her hand up and down his shaft, loving his sharp intake of air as she passed her thumb along the small opening on the tip. Alexis wanted to feel him lose control more than she wanted her next breath. Something animalistic had unleashed inside her and it wanted to run free.

"Get rid of my panties, Cliff."

The hand that had so thoroughly played her body moved to her hip and tightened. Alexis was sure that she'd have a bruise in that spot come morning. He released his clenched fist of her hair to place it on her other hip. The material shredded apart with only a pinch of her skin.

"I want to taste you," Cliff growled against her mouth, but she shook her head slightly. "Later, I need you inside me right now."

With one strong arm, Cliff wrapped it entirely around her waist and lifted her slightly. The tip of his cock slipped along the wetness of and sex. As she hovered above him, she rocked her hips as she had done against his hand, her body growing wetter with each pass.

Through clenched teeth, Cliff asked, "How long has it been?"

"Too long," she admitted, not telling him it had been over six years. They'll have time for that discussion at a later date, all Alexis was concerned with was finding her next release.

"Go slow, baby," he told her as he loosened his hold on her waist. Immediately she reached out and settled her hands on his shoulders, taking care not to rest any weight on her wounded arm.

Cliff aligned himself at her hot entrance and Alexis slowly lowered herself onto his dick. Inch by agonizing inch. She knew it would hurt as he stretched her body to accommodate his size, but as she continued to take him in, she found herself holding back gasps of pain.

Sensing her change of mood, Cliff slipped his hand between her legs and gently began to rub her clit again. "I'm sorry, sweetheart. It will feel good in a minute." Her body began to relax as the pleasure built slowly.

Finally, after what felt like hours, her thighs touched his as she completely seated herself on his shaft.

"Fuck, nothing had ever felt this good. This perfect."

And she felt the same. Despite the pressure, Cliff made her body feel alive in a way it never had before.

Alexis lifted up just a few inches to relieve the ache building between her legs only to have Cliff grip her waist, holding her in place.

"I need just a minute; otherwise, I'll explode right now."

She tried to hide her smirk, knowing she had this effect on him, that she could bring him to his knees.

"I need to move, Cliff."

Alexis didn't wait for him to respond, the desire overpowering everything else. With slow, steady movements, she raised then lowered herself on his cock, adding a swirl in her hips as she picked up speed.

It was not long before her moves became sporadic and wild, she threw her head back as her body took over.

"Oh, god," she called out as the familiar sensation came into reach. Alexis knew she was just seconds away from going over the edge. "I'm so close."

"Fuck," Cliff growled. He grabbed her hips to hold her in place, then began to thrust upward at an alarming speed.

"Yes. Yes. Yes!" Alexis cried out as an orgasm soared through her, limbs shaking at the onslaught of pleasure. But Cliff's pounding never wavered. He continued to drive into her body over and over until his cock somehow grew even larger before releasing himself deep inside her channel.

She collapsed against him as he fell against the couch, their heavy breaths swirling together. Sweat-soaked bodies slid across each other as they heaved for air in unison.

They stayed silent for a few minutes, allowing themselves to cool down. Cliff ran his fingers through the messy waves of her hair, Alexis didn't even care as he snagged a few tangles. She hadn't felt this free and spent in a long time and she wanted to savor every second.

"Definitely not tired now," she said with her lips pressed against his shoulder, causing him to chuckle.

"Well, what do you want to do, pretty girl?"

Leaning away from his body, Alexis smiled wickedly at the man that had completely entranced her.

"I'd love to take a dip in the lake to cool off."

Wrapping his arms around her waist, Cliff drew her breast toward his mouth.

"Do you now?"

"Yeah," she said breathily. "It would be a way to cool off. And no one will find us there."

"Think you can be quiet?"

Bringing her hand from his shoulders to his face, she pulls him toward her, their lips brushing. "I'm sure you could find a way to keep me quiet."

Chapter Six

A week had passed since Alexis and Cliff gave in to their attraction. Since then, he had spent every night, and some mornings, in bed with her. And with Logan giving her the go ahead to return to normal activity, they had been insatiable. But Cliff worried that the longer that Alexis stayed with him the more emotions he hadn't felt in years would begin to bloom inside him. And those kinds of feelings would make it difficult for him to focus when he needed to protect her.

He had little doubt that her father was coming. Lev wasn't a man that responded spontaneously. No, he would strike with a plan in place, which meant Cliff and the town needed a plan in place too. So far, all the group had decided was to keep an eye on Alexis twenty-four seven.

But it was quiet. Too quiet. And Cliff had been on edge wobbling in the breeze.

The past Tuesday, his new receptionist quit on her second day because he snapped at her while explaining how to add new products into their inventory system. She had duplicated an entry, which Cliff himself had done numerous times, but with his mind elsewhere, he couldn't contain his anger.

Thank goodness for Alexis offering to do the job in the meantime. She claimed to be bored and no surprise quickly picked up the systems.

Wade, his new seasonal artist, had been fitting in well with the shop. He was quiet for the most part and kept to himself, much as Cliff had when he first moved to town. He suspected that the Lady Busy Bees would be cornering him soon to get Wade's life story, whatever hadn't been pulled in his background check. Somehow those ladies got wind of everything.

"You have an appointment in fifteen minutes," Alexis called out as she leaned around the ledge separating his section.

"Tattoo or piercing?"

"Navel piercing."

Sauntering farther into the room, Cliff watched the gentle sway of her hips as she moved to stand in front of him. Damn, he had it bad for this woman. This insatiable hunger for her that couldn't seem to be quenched.

"You know, I thought belly button rings went out of style. Maybe I'm just getting old," she joked.

"Naw, we get them pretty frequently. It's an easy piercing. You know what that means?"

Reaching out, he gripped her hip, tugging her close until she straddled his legs on the chair. Her skirt flounced around them, draping across their laps like a blanket. The heat between her thighs rubbed against his straining cock aching behind his cargo shorts.

"No, what does that mean?

"It means that I don't have to spend these fifteen minutes prepping anything."

Leaning forward, Alexis moved closer until her lips rub against the edge of his ear. Cliff's hands slithered up her skirt until they landed on the globes of her ass.

"What should we do during that time?" Her voice grew husky with each word.

Slipping his fingers beneath the center of her panties, Cliff replied, "I'm sure we can come up with something interesting."

Twenty minutes later, Cliff watched a frazzled Alexis run her fingers through her hair, resetting the ponytail he had gripped as she rode him on the chair. He was pretty sure that the smirk on his face gave them away as they moved out to the waiting area. Alexis doing so at a quick apologetic pace while he sauntered in like he owns the place, because he did and didn't care if everyone knew that he was fucking the life out of Alexis in the back room.

The young woman startled from her perch against the desk where Wade stood keeping her occupied.

"Thanks, man," Cliff acknowledged with a friendly slap on the back. "I'll buy your lunch today."

"Thanks," Wade grunted then moved away from the desk as Alexis skirted behind it.

At first, Cliff thought that he was going to have an issue with Wade being around Alexis. His new hire had this particular look about him whenever she was near, but as the days went on the look drifted away. Now, he barely made any eye contact with her, or with anyone.

"Okay, Dominque, I hear you want a navel ring?"

The barely-an-adult- woman clapped her hands gleefully as she nodded. "Yes! It is my eighteenth birthday present to myself. I promised my mom it wouldn't be a tattoo yet, but my cousin, Tamara, and I are working on her. Tamara said you are the very best and if someone is going to shove a needle through my skin, I want the very best," the woman said in one breath.

Tamara was the pharmacy technician working down the street at Everleigh Connelly's pharmacy. She'd been coming in for years to add to a design she had wrapped around her ribs. He was pretty proud of the piece.

"Sure, now while I set up the booth, Alexis here is going to go over the aftercare paperwork. It will be just a minute and I'm sorry about the wait."

"Thanks! And no apologies. Sometimes love takes us over," she said with a wistful expression.

It wasn't love, but lust had the same effect.

Just as Cliff finished pulling the equipment from the autoclave, Wade peeked his head into the booth. "Hey, I need to take a phone call. I'll be out back."

"Sure."

Cliff didn't feel the need to micromanage the seasonal staff. They were more than just temporary help; they were valuable to his business.

After setting up the tray with sterilized equipment, Cliff returned to the waiting area and motioned for Dominique to follow him back. Her dark brown skin was a stark contrast to the silver clamp. It was a beautiful shade that he may try to replicate by mixing ink colors later.

"Alright, you're going to take a deep breath, then when I tell you to, you'll release it at the same time I set the piercing. Sound good?"

"Yes, Mr. Walker."

"You can call me Cliff, sweetheart," he said with a smirk.

"Oh, that must be the smile Tamara was talking about. Said you could melt panties off a nun."

Well, that was an unexpected compliment.

Ignoring her statement, Cliff instructed her to take a deep breath, then at the release, he pierced the needle through the skin. A small hook piercing followed the needle and in two minutes, Dominique's birthday present was complete.

"Wow, that didn't hurt at all. You're really good, Cliff. Thank you."

"You're welcome. I'm going to clean up here and Alexis will ring you out upfront. And make sure you come to me when you and Tamara convince your mom for that tattoo."

The thin woman swung her legs off the table. "Will do." As she waved goodbye Cliff began to clean up his station. He knew that after lunch he had two tattoo appointments. Luckily, they were both small and common designs by new clients.

Grabbing his phone, he sent a text to Harlan and Ryker Connelly to see if either of them wanted anything added to their pieces. He had an itch to design, and though he drew during his downtime, he liked it when it had a purpose and didn't just sit in his portfolio.

Back out front, he watched Alexis wave goodbye to Dominique before turning her gaze toward him. His heart started pounding in his chest as she smiled as if he was the sunlight during a storm.

"When was your birthday?" Cliff randomly asked, earning himself a confused gaze and tilt of her head.

"Um, November seventeenth. Yours?"

"April fourth."

"What is this? Twenty questions?"

"No, just curious," he pointed out. Stepping up behind her, Cliff placed his hands on either side of her body on the desk. Rubbing his nose along her neck, he asked, "Do you have anything against tattoos?"

Her voice was breathy as she replied, "No."

Pressing his lips against the skin where her neck met her shoulders, he licked and nipped along the exposed skin just above her shirt, moving to the other side. Anger burst inside him as he took in the red and purple wound braising her shoulder, the dark lines of her sutures still visible. This was one of the first days she'd been able to go without a dressing on it.

"You have beautiful skin," Cliff told her, though his eyes remained on the nasty scar that she will eventually have. Though, to him, the injury would only make her more beautiful.

"Thanks. I just never know what to get, it was not that I never wanted one."

"You'd probably want to start with something small first, but I'd love to put feathers along your shoulder blades."

"Feathers? Why?" she asked curiously.

"To show that you have risen above it all." He peppered one last kiss on her shoulder then stood straighter, twisting her in his arms.

"That sounds nice." She smiled up at him, her arms wrapping around his waist.

Cliff bent forward and kissed her softly. "Can I take you to lunch today?"

"I thought you were going with Wade," she responded, her lips moving against his.

"I'm sure that I can make it up to him. I'd rather have your company."

Pulling back, Alexis' smile widened as if he'd fixed all that was wrong in the world. Damn, he loved it.

"I'd love to join you."

"Good. I'll just let Wade know."

Cliff hurried to the back of the shop and opened the door. Whatever Wade had been discussing on the phone ended abruptly. Cliff couldn't pinpoint it, but something about Wade staring at the ground had his hackles rising.

"Hey, I'm going to take Alexis to lunch, can we postpone?"

"Sure thing."

Cliff took a heavy breath and the scent of marijuana lingered in the air. Now, the secretive conversation made sense. "Wade, I have a zero-tolerance policy with drugs. If I catch you using or selling, I'll have to let you go."

"Sorry, boss. Just letting off some steam. Got into it with my girl this morning."

Something about his explanation seemed fishy, but what did Cliff know about girl problems? He and Alexis had moved from barely acquaintances to whatever they were doing. Were they in a relationship? Was she just biding her time with him until she could return to her home?

The back door closed behind Cliff as he turned back around. Now that the questions were in his mind, he couldn't seem to shake them free.

"Cliff, are you ready?" Alexis asked, standing at the end of the hallway, her beautiful smile beckoning him forward.

Yeah, he was ready; he'd take whatever he could with her.

With his hand wrapped around hers, they walked down Main Street. Alexis being here with him was right, he just hated the circumstances that brought her back to Carson.

As they approached the diner, Austin and Nikki exited with their toddler Grace in toe. They swung her in the air as she took a leap off the sidewalk. Cliff never imagined having children, he always felt that he had seen too much hatred in the world. How could he possibly give someone all of the love and care that they deserved? It was the same reason why he wasn't sure where this thing with Alexis may go.

"Hey, guys," Austin waved as they stepped closer on the sidewalk. Cliff and Alexis replied in the same manner.

"I'm sorry to hear about the trouble you're in, Alexis. Please let us knew what we can do to help. With all you've done for our family we've claimed you as our own," Nikki said, her hand gently reaching out to clasp Alexis'. Cliff looked over and swore that he saw tears in Alexis' eyes. He would hate for Nikki to upset her, but the Connelly's had always been the kind to bend over backward to help someone.

But Alexis surprised him as she released his hand and wrapped Nikki in a hug. The women stood together in their embrace for a few minutes leaving Cliff and Austin staring at each other awkwardly. It was not that Cliff didn't like Austin; he just didn't know him very well.

"So, uh. . .do you need any help renovating your cabin?" the man asked as he lifted his daughter into his arms.

"Actually, I need to look at replacing the siding. I wanted the shingles to last as long as possible, but last year's snowstorm took its toll on them."

"Sure, just call my office and we can set something up. I'd love to come check it out. Last time I was out that way, Nikki and I used the lake-" A nudge in Austin's ribs left him sputtering. Cliff didn't imagine what those two were doing at his lake. It was no secret what a lot of people did in the back of his property. Thankfully that stopped when he purchased the land and added the no trespassing signs. He hadn't caught anyone there since.

"Sorry," Nikki said, "We just came to meet Austin for lunch. Grace and I have a playdate with Aunt Avery scheduled."

"Good to see you."

Cliff held open the door to Angie's diner for Alexis to enter then followed her inside, watching in amazement as everyone turned in their seats to stare at them. Not a peep came from a single customer. He had heard of this happening when newcomers came into the diner, but he had never experienced it for himself. His first time had been with Mrs. Connelly and no one asked questions when she was around.

A rush of people moved toward the entrance at an alarming rate, shoving him out of the way to get to Alexis, but he held her hand firmly. Shirley and Temple Fitzgerald were the first to encase Alexis in their arms, quickly followed by the rest of the Lady Busy Bees. The elderly women moved at a speed that surprised him. Glancing around the room he noticed the center tables pushed together to create one long table down the

middle of the diner. They must have been having a
meeting.

He looked over to Alexis surprised to find her
smiling down at the older women as they regale her
with stories and promise to brush up on their shooting
skills to help keep her safe. Cliff wasn't sure if the
women having firearms was safer or more of a
problem.

"Sorry 'bout that," a voice spoke next to him
and Cliff turned to find Angie standing at the front of
one of the booths. "This booth work for you?"

Releasing his hold of Alexis, Cliff nodded at
Angie and slipped onto the vinyl seat. Typically, he'd
go for the back booth to keep an eye on the place, but
right now, he'd take what he could get. He didn't think
Alexis would like being paraded down the aisle for
everyone to stare at.

A few minutes later Alexis slipped onto the seat
across from him, smiling warmly with a flush of red on
her cheeks.

"Sorry about that."

"No need to be sorry," he told her as he lifted
the menu up as if to read, but he already knew what he
wanted. Unlike his Connelly friends, he would eat just
about anything on the menu. The Connelly's each had
their tried and true menu item, and if the meatloaf
special was on the board there was no question what

they would be choosing. He had the entire thing memorized.

"What looks good?" she asked, her eyes darting back and forth across the laminated sheet.

"I'm going to get a Rueben with homemade fries."

"Oh, that sounds good," she exclaimed, setting her menu back on the table.

Cliff leaned back in the booth, extending his legs out before him, placing them on either side of her legs.

"You seem at home here. I can't remember, but did you grow up in Carson?" she asked as Angie stepped up to their table to get their orders. She immediately returned with their two sweet iced teas.

"Nope, I found Carson on a map when I left the Army. Though, I'm pretty certain Carson found me," he joked as he took a sip of the cool drink.

"I know exactly what you mean. I grew up in a small town, not nearly as small as this, but you know what I'm saying. But once I was dropped off at the orphanage I jumped from house to house until I found one that could tolerate me. I was a bit of a pint-sized bully."

"You? I don't believe it."

Laughing Alexis continued, "I had to be, otherwise everyone would take advantage. I was lucky. None of the homes were too bad. Some were overfilled, some really wanted a certain age or gender. It just took finding a good fit. Being older in the system was hard, especially when you can remember your parents and wish for them to come get you every day. Made it hard to form attachments."

"I get it. Truthfully, being in the Army was the same way. Never knew when you would get picked up or moved. If you did go home, you never knew for how long. And it wasn't just the soldier that suffers." Cliff cast his eyes downward as an image of his ex-wife came to mind.

Trying to lighten the mood Alexis changed the subject. "So, tell me how you got into tattooing."

After lunch Cliff and Alexis walked back to the shop, but as they passed by the abandoned bar with the dumpster out front, Cliff stopped. He peeked through the dirty window, wiping away some grime with his forearm. Surprise gripped him. A man stood in front of a plaster covered column, ramming a sledge hammer against it over and over. The man wore a mask so that only his dust-covered dark hair could be seen. Each swing was meant for more than just demolition, he could sense the pain in the man's strike. After one more hit, an avalanche of plaster and wood boards came crashing down, leaving a column of old exposed brick.

"Well, damn," Cliff murmured, shocked at what was hiding beneath the tattered exterior of the column.

"What?" Alexis asked from behind him.

"I think I need to introduce myself to our new neighbor."

"Well, maybe you can do that tomorrow. You have an appointment in a few minutes."

Smirking, Cliff wrapped an arm around her shoulder and pressed a kiss on the top of her head. He wanted nothing more than to be able to keep her, to make her his. But he had no idea how to give her the kind of life that she would be worthy of.

***

Alexis thought she loved her job. Seriously, it was why she put up with so much and willingly took any case handed to her. But after working at Cliff's shop for a week, Alexis was beginning to reconsider her stance. The danger, the bullets, the criminals – they all were what made her wake each morning. Working as an office manager and receptionist of sorts wasn't something she spent all her years at college to put on her resume. Regardless, spending time with a man who was so artistically brilliant, and sexy as all get-out, made her days much more enjoyable.

There was something about Cliff. She couldn't place her finger on it or narrow it down, but he shifted something inside her. Something she never knew she needed or craved – affection.

When he carried her into the shop after she was wounded, he was so caring, so thoughtful to help keep her mind off the pain. Sure, any person with a heart would have done the same, Heath had the entire twenty-four-hour trip, but it was how Cliff did it. It was as if he had been trying to take all her pain into himself.

Wade walked into the reception area with a frown, though Alexis was beginning to wonder if that was how his face looked most of the time. When he first arrived, he had freaked her out a bit. His over-gelled black hair and black eyes gave him a sinister look. He also kept himself decked out in all black, even with the warm summers approaching. She wondered if it was a stage he just never grew out of.

"My appointment is running late. I'm going to the store," he grunted as he stepped out of the shop and turned left down the sidewalk.

Not a man of many words.

Moving back toward Cliff's booth, Alexis stopped at the entrance and watched as he leaned over the woman's hip. Her skirt, which was already three inches too short, sat low enough on her pelvis that Alexis could make out her shaved lady region. Cliff wiped at the black ink with a towel in his hand and Alexis took a moment to interrupt.

"Hey," she whispered and Cliff's gaze immediately darted up to hers, followed by a smile. "Wade went to the store. I just wanted to give you a heads up."

The woman lying on the table grunted at their exchange, obviously upset that Cliff was paying Alexis attention.

"Thanks, babe," he replied and Alexis practically beamed from the top of her head to the tips of her sandal-clad feet.

She watched as he dipped the gun into a small cup of ink and moved back over the client to complete her piece. Alexis loved watching him work, the lines on his face deepened as he concentrated on the small lines.

She was jarred away from the display as the phone to the studio rang. Rushing toward the front of the store, she answered on the fourth ring.

"Carson Ink, how can I help you?" Alexis greeted.

At first, she heard nothing, just silence on the other end, which wasn't unheard of when people called the shop. The town had older phone lines that sometimes took a few seconds to pick up.

"Hello? This is Carson Ink; can I help you?"

"Hello, Alexandra," the gravelly voice replied.

Alexis had never felt fear like she did at the sound of the voice on the other line. Sure, when she was out on a mission, fear always ran through her veins, but it was usually mixed with adrenaline that gave her a heightened sense of power. But the terror she felt at this moment shocked her system – she was frozen in place.

"What. . .what do you want, Father?" Alexis whispered, her throat now as dry as the Sahara Desert.

"I need to ensure that you're not going to be a problem. You know too much and that doesn't sit well with me."

"But, I'm your daughter? Why-" she began but was interrupted by his shout on the other end. "You were a goddamned mistake that your mother should have taken care of. All you were to me was a piece of property that had worn out her welcome.

"I don't understand."

"I never wanted you, that was your mother's wish. I had a business to run and business that your damn existence was ruining. My whore of a daughter allowing a man she barely knows have his wicked way with her body." Alexis gasped at his description of her. How could someone that cruel be of relation to her?

"What? You think I didn't know what you've been doing while you've been in that Podunk little town? Yeah, they threw me off for a while, but I'm coming for you. I have eyes everywhere. And you will give yourself up willingly; otherwise everyone else will pay for your mistake."

"What is wrong with you?" she asked. "Why are you doing this?" Flashes of her teammates falling to the ground during their ambush flickered across her mind and she bit back a cry.

"Payment is due. I'm coming." Her father ended the call before Alexis could fathom what just took place.

He knew everything. Somehow someway, he knew everything.

Alexis' entire body shook as the dial tone sounded. She had rehearsed what she would ever say to her father if he contacted her, even practiced with Cliff, but when it actually happened, she froze on the spot. Instead of the strong independent woman she was, she turned into the scared seven-year-old, wondering why her family abandoned her.

The phone remained firmly gripped in her hand, pressed against her ear as if her father was still on the line. His words ran through her mind on repeat. Mistake. Whore. Payment. How could someone she once loved turn out to be so cruel? But his blood ran through her veins leaving her wondering if she could turn out to be just like her father.

Alexis didn't notice as the client sauntered out into the waiting area, she was too lost in her thoughts to speak, let alone ring someone out on the register

The woman's words were a garbled mess in Alexis' ear. "I think your receptionist is having a breakdown."

From the corner of Alexis's blurred vision, she watched Cliff join the client, then drop his black latex gloves to the ground as he rushed to Alexis' side. He gripped her face in his hands, the phone pressed to her ear fell to the floor with a clang.

"Alexis," he cried out, his gaze moved over every inch of her body. "Are you okay? Are you hurt?" As if remembering the client standing in the room, Cliff turned to her and told her to leave, letting her no there was no charge for the tattoo. It was not until the woman huffed as the door closed behind her that Cliff turned his attention back to Alexis.

"What is it, baby? You look like you've seen a ghost."

Did she? Seen and spoken to a ghost of her memory, only to find out that he was a vicious drug and sex trafficker hell-bent on paying off his debts with Harposia using his daughter as payment.

"Father," Alexis whispered and Cliff's face turned ashen.

"Fuck. Fuck!" he shouted. "On the phone?" he asked and at her curt nod, he released her face and picked the phone off the ground. Alexis watched as he quickly glanced at the calendar on the desk then back at her. "I'm going to call Preston and Dylan, then we're going upstairs. I want you to stay there for the rest of the day, not a single person can get in without me. You'll be safe, I promise."

And she trusted him. He would keep her safe at all costs, and she'd do the same for him. Even considered giving herself up to protect him and this town that had welcomed her with open arms.

Her head was spinning by the time Dylan and Preston marched into the shop. They took one look at her and their expression morphed from carefree to one of anger and rage. Cliff had only told them on the phone that he had some new information. He kept it as vague as possible in case her father and his minions had the town bugged. They couldn't form any other explanation as to how he was getting information.

As they walked toward the back of the shop, leaving Wade in charge, Alexis revealed the short conversation almost word for word.

"Somehow he knew that Cliff and Preston went to Raleigh to throw him off with the locket. How would he have known that without bugs somewhere?" she asked.

"I think we need to make sure that everyone in town is on the up and up. At least until all of this is over," Cliff added.

At the top of the stairs, Dylan rested his hand on Cliff's arm, garnering her protector's attention. "We may want to start thinking about plan b."

Moving until he was a breath away from Dylan, Cliff leaned into his space. "I'm not sending her to witness protection just so some mole in the FBI rats her out. You know as well as I do that the system isn't foolproof. We're going to do it my way, or you can get the hell out."

Holding up his hands in surrender, Dylan took a step back until his back rested along the railing of the steps. "I know, man. I'm just afraid that you're getting too close, that your head isn't in this fully. I want to protect Alexis just as much as you do. She's been my friend for a long time."

Finally speaking up Alexis interrupted the two alpha men. "I'm staying here because it's where I feel safest. If it gets to the point when I feel innocent people are in danger, I will leave."

Cliff shook his head as he opened the door to his studio. "You know that isn't how it works."

"Well, it is going to have to," she told him as she slipped past and into the open room. "Now, tell me what we're doing in here."

"I need to trace the call and find the bugs in town."

The group stared at him, then back down to the six government-issued computers then back to him again. Confusion was clear as day on their faces.

She watched as Cliff opened a small picture frame and placed his hand against a biometric reader on the wall. Before them, a false wall opened up to reveal a room with monitors across every open surface on the wall and one computer set in the middle. Cliff smiled smugly as he waved a hand in front of the room.

"I'm so jealous right now," Preston mumbled as he stepped inside. Dylan nodding his agreement as he followed.

Alexis stepped up to Cliff and wrapped her arm around his waist. He pulled her close, her face rested against the taut muscles of his chest.

"I won't let anything happen to you," Cliff whispered against her hair.

In his embrace, Alexis closed her eyes and nodded – she believed him. They stayed like that for a minute just relishing in the safety and warmth of each other before joining the men inside the room. As Cliff entered, he pressed a red button that shut the door behind him.

"This is pretty swanky," Alexis told him as she walked around the room, looking closely at the monitors. He had a view into every building and space on Main Street, even the newly constructed retirement center near the outskirts of town. "Why do you have all of this?"

"Just in case. I don't come in here unless there is an emergency. It's not for spying, but you never know," he said with a shrug of his shoulders.

Cliff sat in the chair in front of the monitor and as the computer came to life, she could see the program requested a zip code, address, or name.

"Oh my gosh, you can see everywhere."

"For the most part. Like I said, I only use it for emergencies."

Alexis couldn't help but wonder if this was the application he used when he tried to look her up.

"First," he began, "I need to track the phone call." Holding up the phone from the office, Cliff scrolled through the recent calls and cursed when it came up as unknown. Without a word, Cliff brought up another program on the computer and typed in the phone number for the studio. As a list of numbers populated on the screen, Cliff highlighted a select few around the time her father called and requested the system to trace.

Most of the numbers came from Carson or the adjacent towns and counties. But after ten minutes, a few of the numbers pinged to other areas. Mexico City. Tokyo. Raleigh. Ontario. Phoenix. Chicago.

"These are the most likely areas associated with the number your father used. It is a cell phone so we could only trace to the area where the signal came from." Spinning in his chair, he turned to look at Alexis. "So, tell me, which one do you think was your father?"

Alexis stared at the names. Raleigh would be too obvious. Though that was where they wanted to lead him, he would have been too smart to go there himself. She thought back to areas populated by the cartel they had been chasing and known associates. Mexico City and Chicago were the first to pop into her mind. Something about the windy city burrowed in her brain and stuck. She couldn't pinpoint it, but somehow she thought that was where her father was located.

"Chicago. I don't know why, but something about it is sticking in my head."

"All right. Well, let's see what we get." Cliff selected Chicago and ran the program to trace the call from that area at the time they received it at the shop.

"While this runs, I want to talk about what we're going to do moving forward. If we locate Alexis' father, I want someone in here monitoring his movements twenty-four seven. Anyone and everyone. We need to know when he's coming. And at this point, I don't care who knows what I have in here. Her safety is a priority."

"What is the plan if he goes off of our radar?" Preston asked, just as a ping echoed in the room.

Cliff looked down at the screen then pressed a key on the keyboard. The monitors flickered then switched to a view of The Institute of Art.

"We just pray that our instincts are good because I have a feeling this is going to be more difficult than we thought."

Alexis gasped as the screens flashed from face to face of the visitors moving in and out of the museum. They stood there for another twenty minutes while the application searched faces and phone connections.

"There! That's him!" Alexis shouted, reaching across Cliff to smack a key on the keyboard to freeze the screen.

The image was blurry, but she could make out the dark hair with graying temples, phone pressed to his ear. Two giant henchmen flanked him on either side. But it was the eyes that did him in, Alexis would recognize them anywhere – they looked just like hers.

"Good work," Cliff stated as he zoomed in on the image and brought it on all of the screens. "Now, let's see what we're working with."

An hour passed as the four of them watched the application track the number across Chicago and adjoining cities.

"Fuck!" Cliff shouted, breaking everyone away from their monotonous stares.

"What is it?" Dylan asked.

"The trace died. Either he killed the phone about ten minutes ago or he has switched out the SIM card."

"So, what do we do?" Alexis asked, but she was afraid she already had the answer.

"We wait."

Begrudgingly Cliff left her with Preston, who offered to take the first watch while Cliff went to his next appointment. He kissed her forehead and sealed her and Preston into the apartment, making sure to show them where he kept a mini-fridge and food.

She had been curious about his job before, but now that she'd seen this hidden room with eyes on the world, Alexis wanted to know more.

They chat mindlessly, he told her how he still felt like an outsider after living in Carson for three years. That it wasn't until recently that things were less strained between him and the Connelly family. She tried to assure him that once he finally moved on with someone else that the family wouldn't continue to think he stayed in Carson for Sydney.

Around 8 p.m. Cliff came up the stairs with Jameson in tow. He explained that the tech whiz was going to work on setting up the monitors for mobile viewing, that way someone could stay at their house but monitor the program remotely. Now that the phone number was no longer detectable, all the program could go off of was facial monitoring. And within the town of Carson, the application would find her father and his henchman's faces quickly.

After another hour, Cliff and Jameson weren't able to detect any bugs placed in the town. Which Alexis knew meant that someone had been feeding her father information.

"Just remember, if your father can give them something that they desperately need or want, people will do just about anything," Cliff explained as she stomped her foot in frustration. "We know the majority of people here and they're trustworthy. But it's the time of year that outsiders come for the summer season. We can't do background checks on all of them." She understood, but she couldn't fight against the desire to do more. It wasn't just her that she's worried about. She worried for the safety of the people she'd come to know as friends and family.

Leaving Jameson in his own personal wonderland, she and Cliff made their way out back to his truck. He helped her inside the vehicle and before she could blink, he started the engine and headed toward his home.

While locked in the room with Preston, Alexis had a lot of time to think, a lot of time to conjure up ideas and worst-case scenarios. She had driven herself crazy with what-ifs, and only one solution came to mind.

Turning in her seat, she watched as the setting sun shone colors of orange, red, and yellow onto the sky just past Cliff's sharp profile. God, she didn't want to hurt him, she didn't want to be another reason for him to cave into himself again as he had with his ex-wife. She committed his face to memory, took note of every eyelash and bit of scruff on his chin. He was beautiful to her, and for the moment, she was his."

"Can you promise me something, Cliff? "The man startled as she spoke, his shoulders jerked toward his ears. He must have been lost in his own world just as she had been.

"What's that, sweetheart?" he replied, turning to glance at her for a moment, unleashing that devilish smile that she loved.

"If it comes to it, please let me go," she begged knowing how much her words must sting.

"I can't do that," Cliff vehemently declined. His hands tightened on the steering wheel until his knuckles turned white.

"Please, Cliff."

"I can't do that, Alexis. Don't ask that of me," he seethed through his teeth, angering Alexis to the point she shouted, "Why not!"

Braking unexpectedly in the middle of the road, dust flew all around them in a cloud of fury.

"Because I fucking love you," Cliff roared as he shifted the truck into park. Shocked, Alexis stared at him as he unfastened her seatbelt, hauled her over the center console, and settled her onto his lap in the blink of an eye.

She didn't get a chance to respond; her mouth was crushed against his, and as he slid the front seat as far back as it would go, their bodies jerked as it met the end.

"You're mine, Alexis, and I'm not letting you go," he said, brushing his lips against hers. She lost herself in his kiss, in his taste, forgetting all about the danger surrounding them all. Because love made you forget everything.

Chapter Seven

Warmth spread all over his body. Lying on his stomach, arms wrapped tightly around his pillow, Cliff felt the heat from the sun rays glaring through his bedroom window onto his skin. He couldn't remember the last time he slept past dawn; his body was so ingrained with its personal alarm clock that he rarely got the chance to sleep in. But he and Alexis wore each other out the night before.

It had been four days since he confessed his feelings to Alexis, and though he wasn't embarrassed by his profession, he changed the subject anytime Alexis brought it up. Worry settled in the back of his mind that there was no way she could feel the same for him. She's so beautiful and warm while he was a man that was sent by the government to do their dirty work.

"Mmm," he groaned as lips press soft kisses across his bare back.

"Sorry, I couldn't help myself," she claimed as she trailed her hands down his back.

"No need to apologize," he told her as he turned slightly, wrapped his arm around her waist, and tugged her beneath him.

His cock nestled between her thighs, the heat immediately causing his shaft to harden. Cliff returned her kisses by doing the same along her neck as she wiggled under him. Their sweat-soaked bodies from the temperature of the cabin slipped against each other as Cliff rocked his hips against hers. His erection nestling between her thighs.

Slipping one hand between her legs, Cliff wasn't surprised to find her soaked for him. They'd both been in a constant state of sexual desire since his confession.

"God, I love how wet you are for me."

"That's because you're gorgeous," she smirked, trailing her hand across his back to grip his ass. Cliff noticed that she did that a lot; he'd have to make sure to keep up with his squats. "Also, I-" she began but Cliff

207 BEHIND THE LENS

cut her off, knowing that he'd be unable to process whatever confession of love she gave. She may think that she loved him, but she didn't know him at all, only the little things he'd told her. She didn't know of the monsters lurking beneath the surface. Years on the battlefield changed a man – that's what his therapist said. More years spent infiltrating terrorist organizations and underage brothels would do a number on a man.

Gliding a finger deep within her channel, Alexis gasped and seemed to forget whatever it was she planned to say.

"Yes," she moaned, tilting her head back and exposing the column of her neck. Cliff couldn't help himself as he leaned down and suckled at the soft skin, rocking his hand against her clit. His dick throbbed in frustration, but he wanted to make Alexis feel good before he thought about himself.

Needing to get her there sooner rather than later, Cliff added another finger, gliding it into her sex as her walls tightened around him.

"God, you're so good at that. Please, don't stop," she demanded and Cliff smiled against her neck, loving the soft moan vibrating through her chest. He loved making her feel this escape, making her lose herself in another sensation.

Her legs stiffened beneath him and she cried out his name, riding out the last of her orgasm against his hand. Her lips puckered in an oval shape as she closed her eyes, the release washing through her. Cliff wished he had his camera to capture such a beautiful vision.

Finally, as her body relaxed against him, Cliff slipped his hand free, bringing it to his lips. He sucked the two fingers in his mouth, captivated by her taste. She had a flavor unlike anything he'd ever tasted and if he could bottle it up, he would. Her eyes glazed over as she watched him indulge in her essence.

Fuck, this turned her on.

Unable to hold back, Cliff moved his legs between her, then entered her in one quick thrust. His curse echoed in the room at the same time her moan reached his ears.

"Goddamn," he bellowed as he pulled back until just the head of his cock rested inside her sex. He repeated the motion again, loving how Alexis mewled. "This is going to be hard and fast, sweetheart," he told her, barely holding on to his last thread of control.

"Fuck me, Cliff."

Damn, he didn't have to be told twice.

"Hold on," he told her, and the smart woman reached behind her and gripped a wrought iron pole of his headboard.

Sitting back on his heels, he lifted her hips in the air and thrust deep inside her channel. She was so slick and hot that Cliff was afraid he'd let go of his release too quickly. Her body was pure decadence beneath him.

Like an unleashed wild animal, Cliff's movements became hurried and maniacal. Alexis' cries of pleasure spurred him on. Leaning down, he captured her mouth in a kiss, their tongues exploring the caverns of each other's mouths.

Alexis' heels dug into his ass and all too soon Cliff began to feel tightening in his balls. Rocking his hips forward, Cliff made sure his pelvis hit her most sensitive spot.

"Oh god, I'm coming," she cried out just as Cliff released himself deep within her core. Her waves of pleasure quickly followed, the sweet walls pulsated and squeezed his cock.

Resting his forehead against hers, their heavy pants mingled in the air between them. They had a connection, one that Cliff couldn't deny, and when their bodies came together like this, he completely lost himself.

"Mmm," she mumbled beneath him, squirming her hips with his cock still settled deep within her body. "What a way to start the morning."

Cliff rocked his hips gently, unable to control the urge to stay nestled in her channel, only to realize that he was still hard and growing with every second.

"I'm thinking about breakfast in bed," he told her and thrusted his hip so that his cock slid all the way to the hilt.

"Genius," she moaned, her hand grasping his back, the short nails digging into his skin.

Yeah, a second helping was precisely what they need.

Their bodies were completely soaked after an hour of Cliff worshipping her a second time. He helped her stand on wobbly legs, her gentle and sated smile beaming up at him as he wrapped his arm around her waist.

"I think I'd like to take a shower."

"Okay, I'll strip the sheets and get them washed. I can clean myself with the outdoor shower."

Her eyes lit up at the mention of the outdoor facility, but he chuckled while balling up the saturated sheets. "It's cold water only."

Her nose and mouth puckered in disgust. "Ew, I'll stick to hot water, thanks."

"I figured as much. I'll make us some lunch."

She nodded as she stumbled toward the bathroom, using her arm to guide her down the wall. He'd heard of fucking someone senseless, but he'd never seen it before, until now.

The cold water was just what he needed, and by the time he came inside, he felt refreshed. The shower was located at the back of the house with a clear view of his monitoring system through the window. He hadn't designed it that way, but some things work out as they're supposed to.

Rummaging through the kitchen, Cliff found that he was lacking in some essential food – like practically everything. He'd have to make a trip to the store. Finding some deli meat and cheese, he grabbed the last pieces of sliced bread and made them some sandwiches.

Unable to sit still, Cliff took his sandwich to the couch and flipped on the television. A national news station popped up on the screen, but Cliff changed it to a sports station to catch up on the baseball scores.

"Thanks," Alexis said as she entered the living room with the sandwich in hand. Alarm vibrated down every column of Cliff's spine. He never heard the water turn off from her shower, or her footsteps down the hall. Damn, he was slipping up, and he couldn't let that happen. Next time it could be something worse than Alexis sneaking up on him.

"You, okay?" she questioned as she took the seat next to him, curling her legs underneath her. Trying to ease her worry, Cliff used his free arm to wrap around her shoulders and tug her close.

"Yeah, I'm good," he lied, hating how each word burned his lips.

"You know. . .I'm a Yankees fan."

Mocking shock, Cliff pushed Alexis away causing her to almost spill her sandwich on the floor.

"No way. You can't be in this house and like the Yankees." Cliff shot daggers in her direction, doing his best to keep his laugh in check, but he failed miserably. One chuckle happened first, then it was quickly followed by a few more. "I'm just kidding, get back here," he said with his arm open wide, gesturing for her to nestle her sweet body against him. Reluctantly she crawled her way back over to him, perching her body against his. "Now, if you were a Red Sox fan, that would be a whole other story."

A knock sounded on his cabin door in the middle of a romantic comedy Alexis picked out after the sports channel moved to a different topic. He hated to admit that he was very intrigued to find out if the girl took the guy back after his fifth failed attempt at a date.

With a grunt, Cliff moved from beside Alexis, hating the loss against his side as he moved toward the front door. He paused in the hallway and muttered a curse. This was the second time today he was so focused on Alexis that he didn't have his mind straight. He should have heard the car approach the cabin, or the alert from the security system. And looking down at his phone, he scrolled through seven alerts. If he couldn't get his act together, Cliff may have no choice but to follow Dylan's plan b, even after he had promised her that he would keep her by his side.

At the door, he greeted Preston, who slowly stepped over the threshold before addressing Cliff.

"Do you know why I'm here?"

"No. Unless you've captured her father, then we should go celebrate."

"Unfortunately, that's not the case. Not a single precinct across the country has got a tag on him. He's either invisible or has a lot of guys in blue working for him."

"Okay, then what brings you by on my only day off from the shop?"

"I need you to turn on the news," the officer said vaguely.

On numb feet, Cliff walked toward the living room with Preston following closely behind. In the jumbled mess of his mind, he could make out Alexis asking what he's doing as he stole the remote from her hand and changed the channel.

A red banner scrolled across the bottom of the screen displaying that six girls between the ages of twelve and nineteen went missing in Asheville, North Carolina within the last week. The girls all resided in a small suburban town on the outskirts of the city closest to the highway leading to Carson.

"Do you think. . ?" Alexis left her question hanging in the air.

"I learned this morning that there was something left at the home of each of these girls. They were targeted specifically," Preston explained, dread crawling up like spiders on his back.

"What was it?" Alexis' small voice inquired, her eyes never leaving the television screen.

"A heart-shaped locket. Identical to yours."

"Dammit!" Cliff shouted in the room, throwing the remote against the wall in his fury. "He's coming for her, and we don't have much time."

"Look, I know not everyone trusts me here, and I get it. I hurt one of their own doing my job. But I think we should let him come," Preston said. "Alexis doesn't want to live her life always looking over her shoulder and if we are just waiting for someone to find him, then we could be waiting forever."

"You want to use her as bait," Cliff seethed.

"It's not a bad idea," Alexis added, her voice stronger than before. It was the powerful FBI agent in her spurring forth and damn if Cliff didn't find that sexy as hell.

But his heart won out. "I can't let you do that."

"You don't have a choice. I don't want to constantly wonder. It was one thing to think we could trip him up somehow, but now we know he's close by. We could use that to our advantage. He thinks so little of women, so little of me; he would never suspect that we have the one up on him."

"I don't like it," Cliff growled.

She strutted over to him, her small hands reaching up and resting on either side of his face. The gentle touch of her thumbs rubbing against his cheeks instantly soothed him.

"Cliff, I love you. I need you to trust me just as I've trusted you."

Tilting his head toward hers, he captured her lips in a soft kiss, savoring the sweet words that she just spoke.

"You love me?" he asked, his lips brushing against hers.

"I do."

Nodding, he pulls her close, regretting that he held her back from saying those three words until now. He had been on edge waiting, but not wanting to know if she felt the same as him.

He took a deep breath, the fragrance of her shampoo filling his lungs. Gazing at the picture across from him, he stared at the image of Alexis across the field.

"I am more than you bargained for."

"No, you're everything," she whispered in reply.

***

"I forgot how much I loved their house," Alexis explained as Cliff helped her exit the truck.

With Preston's guidance, Cliff and Dylan called an emergency meeting after learning that her father was making a statement. But even though it was a weekday, Mrs. Connelly took the opportunity to turn a quiet get together it into a barbeque. And the entire town was invited.

Cliff had stopped at the store on the way to pick up a potato salad and a bouquet of flowers for Amy, which made them a bit later than everyone else. They were parked five houses down from the Connelly's driveway. Luckily, they didn't seem to be the only ones late to the party as a few other stragglers, that Alexis didn't recognize, fell in line behind them.

What she wouldn't give to be able to settle down in a nice neighborhood like this on the outskirts of a small town. She hated to admit it, but one of her favorite channels was a home and garden network. Whenever one of the shows focused on small towns, she found herself glued to the television. She knew that it was nothing more than a dream, but being here with Cliff made it seem so real and within her grasp.

Together they walked hand in hand up the paved driveway, stepping onto the large porch. Alexis took a moment to admire the wooden planks resting against the brick house with tons of handprints of various sizes. She reckoned that they must belong to Amy and Joseph's kids and grandchildren.

Before Cliff could knock, Amy opened the door wide and ushered them inside. She tugged Cliff into her arms, and then did the same with Alexis, before taking the flowers and side dish. While Amy greeted the others on the porch, Alexis took a moment to look around the foyer. It was formal, yet cozy. The perfect mix of the petite woman with a sophisticated blonde haircut and her rustic husband. With a keen eye, Alexis examined some of the knickknacks and pictures more closely. There was so much love and warmth in the room that it was practically overflowing with devotion.

The group followed Amy toward the back of the house and through the open door leading to a well-groomed back yard. A gathering of kids played on a large wooden playground while the parents stood by chatting with each other.

Alexis moved to follow behind Cliff, but Amy called out her name and asked her to help place the flowers in the vase. Though she didn't know much about being a mother, Alexis knew the signs of trying to get someone alone to talk. Amy was about to host her own intervention.

Using a stool, Amy rummaged through one of the upper cabinets above the refrigerator before locating a slender yellow vase. Alexis took the flowers and unwrapped them on the counter by the sink.

"You're planning on leaving him, aren't you," Amy said as she took a pair of kitchen shears and began to cut the flowers' stems down to size. The tone in her voice wasn't a question; she's stating it as if she knew what had been running through Alexis' mind since she learned of the children's kidnappings.

Not wanting to add fuel to the fire by lying, Alexis nodded and looked out the window as she said, "Yes, ma'am."

"I thought you were smarter than that."

Surprised, Alexis turned her gaze back to Amy to find the woman still working on the stems.

"Pardon me?"

"You're going to run away. Your plan was to leave so that your father would follow you and leave us alone. Am I close?"

Swallowing her tongue, Alexis could only nod. Somehow this small town mother hit the nail right on the head.

"You see that man right there? The one chatting with my husband?" Alexis glanced out the window again, her eyes searching until they landed on Cliff and Joseph. Subconsciously she mimicked his wide smile. "The first year he lived in Carson, he only answered in grunts. For a while, I thought he couldn't speak, but then as he got to know some of us, he opened up. Now, Cliff isn't one to say a lot in general, but we got to know and love the man as if he were family.

"Then, you came along. From the moment he first saw you something inside of him changed. You being here has brought out the man he always deserved to be. Do not take that from him."

"But. . ."

"No buts. You both are worthy of more than you've been given in this life, don't give up on it yet. Fight. See him the way that he sees you."

She let Amy's words sink in. Maybe she was being a coward by leaving. And knowing that there wasn't any guarantee that her father would leave everyone in the town alone was a big question mark hanging in the air. For all she knew, he may take out the town just in spite of her.

"I'm so confused," Alexis confessed.

"Love will do that to you. Now, if you don't mind. I'm going to get this shindig started and you are going to let everyone help come up with a plan that involves you staying."

"Yes, ma'am."

She smiled as Amy pat her shoulder while walking out to the yard. From the kitchen, she watched as Joseph engulfed his wife in his arms, his love for her shining through with every touch and smile. Cliff looked up her way and the corners of his lips tilted upward as their eyes met.

She did love him and Amy was right; she'd be an idiot to give this up. Walking toward him, Cliff met her halfway, leaning down to brush his lips against hers.

"I love you."

Repeating his words, Alexis said, "I love you too."

"Are you sure that it's not too short?" Alexis asked as she stared at her reflection at the town salon named Clipped. Shaking her head, her once long wavy tresses brushed the top of her shoulders.

Behind her, the Connelly women beamed in the mirror. Cassidy, Sydney, Everleigh, Avery, Nikki, Norah, and Poppy formed a semicircle around the worn leather chair.

"It's gorgeous."

"I want to cut mine like that."

"No way."

"I'm so jealous."

"That is perfect."

The compliments rung out from their smiling faces and Alexis couldn't help but glance at herself once more.

The first step of the plan the group concocted at the Connelly's barbeque was to give Alexis a makeover of sorts, even though she was pretty sure the women forced that point because they were itching at the bit to get their hands on her for girl time.

"How will this help bring out my father?" she asked them and as their eyes darted off to various points of the room, she had her answer. "You know, if you just wanted to get together, then you could have just asked."

"Except Cliff doesn't let you out of his sight," Cassidy explained.

"So, we had to do something drastic. This seemed like the best bet. And we wanted a chance to get you alone so we could learn all about what you've been doing to occupy your time," Nikki added, definitely pinning herself as the most devious of the group.

The girls began peppering her with questions about her love life before and after Carson, laughing when she answered them with a question of her own.

"What love life?"

The shop owner, Kelsey, a young woman with cropped hot pink hair, closed and locked the front door, then proceeded to hand out glasses of Champagne to the group. At Avery's decline, the woman handed her a bottle of water.

She joined their group just as Everleigh questioned Alexis about Cliff. She couldn't help herself, never being "one of the girls," this feeling of being part of a tribe was something she'd craved since she was younger.

"He's. . .just. . .incredible. I don't have any other words to describe it. I mean, I knew that there was this passionate man lying beneath his hard surface, but I definitely underestimated him."

"And how is the sex?"

"Wait," Nikki called out, setting down her glass and grabbing a notebook from her purse. "I want to write this down; it may go in my next book. And please feel free to be as detailed as you want." She winked at Alexis causing her to laugh, the glass of wine sloshing over the edge of the glass.

"He's an amazing lover. And not that I have many to compare him to, but I can say with certainty he will always be at the top of the list. He always makes sure that I'm taken care of at least once or twice before we get to the good stuff, you know? Foreplay is never forgotten."

"Ah, foreplay is the best. I can't believe so many men try to skip over it. Like, if you want a blow job, I want you to play with my pussy and finger fuck me, am I right?" Sydney announces to the group, startling them all into silence. Whenever they're together Alexis always noted how quiet she seemed around her family. Maybe the sips of Champagne were loosening her up. Sydney glanced around the room, taking in the women's stared.

"You," Alexis said, breaking the silence as she pointed via the mirror to Sydney, "Are abso-fucking-lutely correct." They shared a smile and the group began sending more questions her way about Cliff, Alexis answering as many as she could.

"You know that isn't his real name – Cliff," Kelsey pointed out drawing confusion from the women. Alexis was aware of that fact, but apparently, she and Kelsey are the only ones. And now she couldn't help ponder how the bright-haired beauty knew.

"Do you know what it was?"

"I know he never looked like a Cliff."

"I swear that man is as mysterious as Pandora's box."

Turning in her chair, Alexis ignored everyone's chattering and looked at Kelsey who stood beside her. "How do you know?" Something inside her tightened as she asked. Something that Alexis didn't want to pinpoint, but could only describe it as an underlying hatred. Was this what jealousy felt like? Surely Cliff and

Kelsey didn't have a relationship like the one that she had with him.

"Oh. . .Oh!" Kelsey's eyes widen as she began to understand the uncertainty in Alexis' question. "Cliff and I. . .no way. . .My uncle is the leasing agent for this building. I don't even know what it is, just that it is not signed to a Cliff."

Her relief was instant and as she took a shuddering breath, she realized that she was farther into things with Cliff than she initially thought. She was all in hook, line, and sinker.

The women stayed and sprinkled her with more gossip and stories as Kelsey twisted up Alexis' hair in thin pieces of tinfoil. She was sure that if she stood outside, she'd get reception from Asheville. While she waited for the highlights to set, she made a plan with Sydney and Dylan to use the shooting range in town to practice. Though she had been in the all-clear from Logan regarding her shoulder, she had been wary of using it as she had before, relying on her non-dominant arm to do most things. But now that her father was closing in, she wanted to make sure that she was up to par with her skills.

A timer on the vanity sounded and Kelsey helped to unravel the metallic mess from Alexis' locks, smiling as each light brown wave came spiraling down. When her head was set free, Kelsey guided her over to the sinks to wash and shampoo the dye from the strands then took her back to the vanity for some styling.

Alexis wouldn't admit it, but as she looked at herself in the mirror, she liked what she saw. She couldn't let the girls have the pleasure of knowing that tidbit. Kelsey put a slight curl in her mane and the caramel highlights set off her naturally tanned skin. The color made her eyes look wide and bright, or maybe that was from the earlier thoughts of Cliff.

After the styling, Cassidy had pulled out a plastic container that Alexis hadn't seen since the late 1990s and began contouring and highlighting Alexis' freshly cleansed skin.

What stared back at her in the mirror was nothing short of a miracle. She couldn't remember ever wearing more than a swipe of mascara, the thought of the makeup aging her always at the back of her mind. But what Cassidy had done made Alexis look young and refreshed. And her hair only complimented it.

"Now, for the dress," Cassidy stated as she closed the lid of the container.

"What?"

Everleigh stepped forward with the red dress Alexis had admired from the stack Cassidy had brought to Cliff's home. She had complained that she had nowhere to wear the beautiful garment.

"You didn't think we'd let you get all dolled up and have no place to go, did you?"

"I just thought. . ."

"Well, Cinderella, you thought wrong. Come on now, your prince awaits."

Shocked, Alexis looked around the room, meeting the knowing gazes of the women she hoped to call friends. "You all set me up."

Piping in, Norah said, "Yeah, we're really good at that. Come on. I can't wait to see the look on Cliff's face."

"Oh god, I'm going to need more than hair and makeup," Alexis exclaimed. Her heart pounded inside her chest, sounding like a freight train to her own ears.

"What, why?" Cassidy asked as she took the dress from her sister.

"Because I've never been on a date."

She was going to throw up. Alexis was going to upchuck every morsel of her lunch all over this gorgeous red dress and black strappy shoes that were by far the prettiest things she'd ever had on her feet.

Standing on the sidewalk outside of the salon, Alexis shifted from foot to foot as she waited with the gaggle of women behind her, their glasses of wine still firmly held in their grasps.

"Guys, I can't do this," she told them, turning around and trying to push past them to go back inside the building.

"You can, little ninja. You can and you will," Cassidy told her as she gripped Alexis' shoulders and turned her back around. "Besides, your man is pulling up now."

With her eyes downcast, she allowed her friend to push her back to the front lip of the sidewalk as an unfamiliar grey sedan pulled up in front of her. Confused, Alexis took in the sleek lines of the Porsche Panamera and wondered who had parked front of her, until the driver's side door swung open, revealing a slacks-wearing ex-Army Ranger.

Cliff.

She almost didn't recognize him with his dark hair slicked back, a light blue dress shirt pulled tightly against his chest with the sleeves rolled up to his elbows and light gray slacks. She was rendered speechless as he moved to stand in front of her. Cliff was by far the sexiest man she'd ever met or had the pleasure of laying eyes on, but him dressed up took his appeal to a whole other level. Damn, he was panty-melting.

"Wow," she breathed out, Cliff smirked at her assessment.

"You look beautiful, Alexis." Reaching up, he grazed the back of his hand across her cheek in a touch so gentle it was as if he was afraid she'd disappear into thin air.

Their gazes met and Alexis couldn't look away, she was pulled to him with a force that she'd never known - it was electric.

"Damn, I think I just came," one of the women murmured. Nikki, she presumed. The women all joined in confirmation.

"Let's get to dinner, sweetheart."

With a gentle press on her back, he escorted her to the passenger side of the car and helped her slide onto the luxurious bucket seats. As he moved around the front of the vehicle, Alexis smiled as she took in the way his pants cupped the firm globes of his ass. She really did love his backside.

"I really like what you did with your hair," Cliff mentioned as he moved the car onto the street.

"Thanks. I was tricked, as you know."

"Not all surprises are bad ones."

"True. So, tell me, where did you get this car?"

"I just borrowed it. It seemed like the occasion warranted a nicer vehicle than the truck."

He appeared almost embarrassed at the admission and Alexis couldn't help but reach over and grip his forearm. Cliff released his hold on the steering wheel and turned his hand over, interlacing their fingers together.

"I prefer you with the truck," she told him, hoping to ease his discomfort. "It suits you."

The car maneuvered over the winding roads taking them out of town and further into the mountains, Alexis admired the trek through the forest and meadows. As they approached a valley between the mountains, a large wooden and stone structure came into sight and Alexis gasped in awe at the enormousness of the place.

"This was where Avery and Logan had their first date. I thought that maybe it was good luck. I hope that it is okay," he explained as he parked the car in the gravel-filled lot.

"It's more than okay. I can't wait to see the inside."

Whatever she had expected before, this was not it. The room, though cavernous and dark, gave a sense of warmth and intimacy in the space. She was amazed at the luxurious offerings the winery and restaurant provided.

She and Cliff sampled the filet mignon and pecan-encrusted halibut for dinner, both of them exclaiming each bite as the best. They split a dessert of chocolate mousse and the creamy texture was so decadent that Alexis continued to steal extra bites when Cliff wasn't looking.

"Are you having a good time?" he asked nervously, the tips of his fingers running circles around the condensation of his water glass.

"I'm having a great time. I. . .ugh. . .have a confession to make."

His ears perked up as the spinning on his glass stopped. "Really? What's that?"

"I've. . .never been on a date before." Taking a deep breath, she rushed out, "I cannot believe I just told you that."

"No, I'm glad. I don't want any secrets between us. And I find that fact hard to believe."

"Hard to believe, but true. Dates when you work all of the time are few and far between."

"That makes sense, I suppose."

"Now, I do believe you said no secrets."

"True, I did," he said clasping her hands in his from across the table. "I promised myself that I would wait until a better time, but I think we should get it out of the way now."

Alexis gripped Cliff's hands tighter, both worry and excitement cresting in her veins. The conversation at the salon ran in her mind and she hoped that he'll finally tell her what his actual name was. She hadn't wanted to ask, afraid that it was a soft spot for him, wanting to wait for him to tell her himself, but curiosity had been eating away at her.

"Sure."

She held her breath, anticipating his secret, wanting to have an authentic look of surprise.

"Dylan, Preston, and I. . .we think you should work for Logan at the clinic until your father appears."

Chapter Eight

It had been five days, seven hours, and thirty-four minutes since Alexis stopped speaking to him. After their date and his suggestion that she work in disguise with Logan at the clinic, she had argued vehemently on the car ride home, but he wasn't changing his mind. He promised her that it was only temporary, but he knew she didn't believe him. He didn't believe himself either.

Between her bout of curses and name-calling Cliff tried to explain that she could easily blend in at the location with the scrubs and mask as needed. When Logan had suggested it, Cliff saw a way to protect her that he hadn't before. He was actually willing to use the assistance of others. Didn't she see how big of a step that was for him? Apparently not, because for the fourth night in a row, he woke on the couch.

God, he missed waking with her in his arms, with her body curled up against his, their slow breaths working in unison. It wasn't just the sex or the intimacy, he just missed her – Alexis, the woman he loved.

"How you hanging, lover boy?" Harlan asked as he slipped inside Cliff's booth at his shop, just ending his stint in the apartment upstairs, monitoring the town.

"She still isn't speaking to me."

"That sucks."

"Yeah," Cliff shrugged as he turned back toward his drawing table in the corner of the room.

"Want me to get Cassidy to talk with her?"

"Naw, that's okay. Logan sends me updates, and as long as she's safe there and home with me, that's all I need."

"Cliff," his friend bellowed.

"So, you want a touch up on your color," Cliff asked, hoping to change the subject.

Harlan plopped himself on the table and tore his shirt up and over his body.

"Yeah, I could use some on my chest."

"Sure, let me get the list of colors and we'll get started."

Twenty minutes later, Cliff wiped away the remains of the ink with a paper towel then cooled off the wound with some ointment.

"This should last a good while unless you plan on standing under the stage lights shirtless again."

"Well. . ." his friend said hesitating while letting his words hang in the air. His and Ryker's band, Exoneration, was going back on tour if his voice was any indication. Cliff wondered if he's told his wife yet.

"No worries, you know I've got you. Let me just shoot a text to Logan for an update, then I'll dress it up."

"Sure."

Taking off his latex gloves, Cliff grabbed his phone from the desk and typed out a text to his friend, just to check that Alexis was okay."

Usually, Logan responded right away with an automated text that he was with a patient or he replied personally. But when Cliff's text went unanswered ten minutes past him dressing Harlan's new ink, Cliff began to worry.

"Hey, man. I'm going to call Logan; he's not answering my message. Then we can go. I'll close early today."

"I'm sure everything is fine, lover boy. But sure, take your time. I'm in no rush."

He called Logan's phone, the doctor waiting three rings until he answered. The time between those three rings seemed like a lifetime.

"You know, I do see patients every now and then."

"Sorry, man. I just had this bad feeling and I wanted to check in. I learned early not to ignore my instincts."

On the other end of the call, Logan explained that Alexis went to take a break, but that she had her phone with her if he wanted to call. But as Cliff eluded that Alexis wouldn't speak to him, Logan chuckled.

"I'll go check to make sure she's okay, hold on."

Through the phone, Cliff could hear the soft patter of Logan's feet as he stepped across the linoleum.

"Cliff, damn man, Cliff she isn't here." The panic rose in his friend's voice. "I saw her go this way. Dude, I'm sorry." Ending the call, Cliff stared blankly at the wall, unsure what his next steps would be.

She's gone. Fuck, she's gone. What to do next? What's the next step?

Harlan must sense Cliff's panic because the large man jumped from the table and stood in front of him.

"Is it Alexis? What do you need us to do? Who do I need to call?"

"I just. . ." Cliff said frantically his hands shoving into his strands of hair as he tried to come to grips with the fact that his woman was missing. "I just need to think for a minute."

"Okay, in the meantime, I'm going to lock your door. And we can get this figured out."

In the blink of an eye, Harlan dipped out of the room and then returned, hands shoved in the pockets of his shorts, chest still bare from the tattoo.

"I need to go up to my apartment and track her."

"Dude, you put a tracking device on her?" Harlan asked as he followed Cliff up the back stairs.

"Yeah. Of course, I did."

"Man, can you put one on Cassidy for me? Just for my own personal satisfaction."

Opening the door to the apartment, Cliff ushered Harlan inside before moving toward the hallway with the enclosed room.

"Let's discuss this after we determine that it works. Sound good?"

The door whooshed open, surprising a bored Ryker.

"Hey, what's going-" the singer began but was cut off as Cliff shoved him in the rolling desk chair out of the way and leaned over the computer, typing in the tracking application.

"There she is," Cliff sighed in relief, then the coordinates of her placement flashed on the screen. Curses sputtered from his mouth as he brought up her whereabouts.

"Where is she?" Harlan asked just as the image of his cabin showed on all of the monitors.

"Home, sorry for all of the worry. I'll take care of this."

Cliff sped around the turns leading to his home, irritation fueling him forward as Main Street wove into rough side roads. Dust and dirt blanketed around his truck as he accelerated on the path, guiding him to his cabin.

How could she be so careless? Didn't she know that he'd been worried sick about her? Maybe having her with Logan was a bad idea, he should have listened to her.

Angry thoughts ran through his mind as he pulled his truck up to his cabin, yanking the door to his vehicle open before it even came to a complete stop.

Cliff marched up the steps, ignoring the fact that the front door to his cabin was wide open.

"Alexis! We need to talk. You can't keep-" he shouted but his words disintegrated into the air as he found Alexis standing in the middle of his living room. Her face was as white as the first snow of the year and her pale lips trembles as they fought to hold back a sob. Blood dripped down from her temple, leaving a path of red on the light green scrubs she wore.

"I'm glad to see that you finally made it," the voice behind Alexis cracked.

Wade.

Cliff should have known that the man he hired would have been behind this. The drugs, the hushed phone calls, his propensity to make Alexis uncomfortable. Despite the clear background check and glowing references, Cliff could only blame himself

A question lingered though. He had hired Wade before Alexis returned to Carson. Did her father convince him to do this just as he had the caregiver at her group home with the necklace?

Unfortunately, Cliff didn't have time to ask as Wade produced a gun and shoved it against Alexis' bleeding skull. Her pain resonated with Cliff as she winced and he wanted nothing more than to pry the gun out from behind his back waistband and take Wade out, but there was a chance that Wade could pull the trigger before Cliff ever got the chance.

The only technique he had in his arsenal was to bide some time. Time for what? He wasn't sure, but he hoped he could convince Wade that this was all a big mistake.

"I'm sorry, I never got the invite," Cliff said casually, doing his best to mask the dread bubbling in his gut. "Come on, man. What are you doing?

"I'm doing what I was born to do. Now, you're going to tell Alexis to leave with me and not put up a fight. If she does, I'll take her straight to the buyer myself. He's very excited to get his hands on her."

"She can hear you, you know?"

"Yes, but our father said she would be difficult. I'm trying to get you to convince her to do otherwise."

Our father?

"Our father. . .?" Alexis asked the question on Cliff's mind, earning herself a hit to the head with the butt of the gun.

"Yes, I'm your half brother. I came here to learn about you before all of this mess. Then when father said you were necessary to close a deal, I knew that I could step in and get the job done."

"This doesn't make any sense," Alexis whispered.

"Sure it does, you'll figure it out soon enough. Or maybe you won't. Father always said that women were a weakness."

Wade shoved Alexis and began to walk toward Cliff, his already panicked state started to rise. Though every ounce of training told him to remain calm and collected, all of that went out the window when someone he loved was in danger.

A plan, he needed a plan. By the dilated look in Wade's eyes, Cliff could only assume that the man was on drugs. As he brought Alexis closer, he could take the small man out, giving her a chance to escape.

"Come on, Wade. I thought that we were friends. I liked having you at my shop," he lied. The man's eyes narrowed into thin slits.

"You were just a means to learn about my sister, about this demon child that should have been taken care of a long time ago. Now she'll serve a purpose and Harposia will stay off our backs letting us run the cartel as we wish." Wade sneered at his sister. "Of course, we do have quite a long journey ahead of us. I'm sure some of father's men will want to make sure the product is up to par."

Red clouded Cliff's vision and fire burned in his veins. Standing here, listening to this man of her own flesh talk about her as if Alexis was nothing more than trash was one of the most disgusting things Cliff had ever witnessed.

A shrill sound broke through the room and Cliff reached into his pocket to get his phone.

"You better make that quick," Wade commanded.

Glancing down at the screen, Cliff held back his sigh of relief when he saw Preston's name. Somehow, he needed to get the officer to realize that something was wrong.

"Hey, Preston. I think that maybe we should get together for beers tonight instead of tomorrow. Heard there was a new bar off the highway on the way to Asheville. Think you could call everyone to meet us there? Great. See you then."

Cliff could only hope and pray that Preston understood what he was trying to tell him because the way Alexis' face morphed meant that she comprehended every word. She knew that he had a plan.

Just as Cliff slipped his phone back into his front pocket, Wade's eyes skipped over to the front window, giving Cliff the second he needed to pull the gun from the back of his pants.

Wade didn't even realize what happened by the time the bullet landed between his eyes. With the drugs in his system, his reaction time was too slow to counter before Cliff obtained the shot.

The sound of Wade's gun dropping to the floor broke Alexis out of her stupor and she rushed toward Cliff, barreling into his arms.

"I'm so sorry," she repeated as she peppered his face with kisses.

As much as he hated it, he pulled her off of his body and cradled her face in his hands. "Babe, you'll have all of the time in the world to apologize, but right now, we have to go."

Gripping her hand, Cliff ran through the living room toward the back door with Alexis trailing behind. Thank goodness for her FBI training and healed leg wound, she was able to keep up with his pace as they flew through the door and over the back deck.

Cliff spared a glance over his shoulder, the large vehicle that had captured Wade's attention now barreling toward the house.

"We need to head toward the lake; there is a path just beyond it leading to Harlan's."

Together they sprinted toward safety, hand in hand. The clearing came into view and Cliff began to breathe a sigh of relief.

"Oh god, they're coming, Cliff!"

At her frantic voice, Cliff peered over his shoulder to find nine men chasing them on foot.

His speed was fast, but with Alexis in tow, he moved a bit slower. He shouldn't have made that mistake. As if these men were part of an Olympic track team, they were closing in on Cliff and Alexis at an alarming rate.

The lake was in view, the path just beyond the marshy bush visible only to a knowing eye.

Taking them toward the left, Cliff diverted from the path and maneuvered them over fallen trees and prickly bushes. The full growth from spring offered them some camouflage. All too soon, the woods came to an end and Cliff made a choice.

Turning toward Alexis, he gripped her shoulders in his hands.

"I love you. I need you to trust me."

"I do trust you."

"Preston should be working to close off the highways, but what I need you to do right now is to run like your life depends on it. I'm going to give you a head start."

"Cliff, no. What are you doing?"

He moved toward the dock jutting out over the lake. Cliff knew that this was her only chance to escape and he'd do just about anything to give her that opportunity.

From the corner of his eye, he watched her dart behind the cattails, tall enough to mask her movements, and head toward the small path on the other side.

Satisfied that she was in the clear, Cliff moved toward the direction of his cabin, ready to occupy these men while Alexis made her break.

Wearing all black, the men stood out as they breached the tree line.

"Good afternoon, gentlemen," Cliff greeted with his gun pointed at the first man that made his appearance. "I hate that you made this trip all the way out here for no reason."

The group of men began to chuckle, and Cliff acted on instinct, pulling the trigger and aiming for the knee of the first man.

"Son of a bitch," the man wailed in pain. "You just wait until I get my hands on that girl. I'm going to tear her part."

"I'm sorry, that isn't going to happen."

"You do realize that this is nine against one, right?" One of the other men called out, but Cliff simply pulled his phone free from his pocket and pressed a button.

A whooshing sound broke through the air, soft enough that only those with the keenest of hearing could make it out. The man fell to his knees, the shocked expression still painted on his face.

In unison, the men began looking around them, up at the trees, down at the ground, but none of them could make out the riggings Cliff had set up. It was set up as a precaution when Alexis came to Carson wounded and barely alive. When he learned that she was his new mission, he knew that he needed something more around his cabin. He never thought he'd need it, but now as Cliff watched a third man fall, he was thankful he had the forethought.

"Now, how many more of these buttons do I have to press before you get the hint. I want you to leave and tell Lev that he's going after the wrong man." Gun still drawn, Cliff peeked a glance down at his phone, looking at which mechanism would spear the man smiling in Cliff's direction. He didn't like the way that the man kept inching closer.

"You could tell him yourself," the smiling man shouted, his smile widening.

"That's okay. I'll-"

Cliff's words die in the air as something hard and blunt collided with the back of his head. Vision blurred and he plummeted down to his knees. The overwhelming pain descended over his body.

Through the haze, he could hear Alexis cry for him. God, he ached to go to her, to tell her that he was sorry for fucking up again, that he loved her more than anything in this world.

But as the blackness closed in, he knew that he'd lost that chance. Through the shrinking lens of consciousness, he pressed one last button on his phone, he just prayed Alexis wasn't caught in the crossfire.

***

Alexis was running for her life, the pain of leaving Cliff to fend for himself wasn't something that she had time to dwell on. A cramp formed on the side of her abdomen and Alexis stopped behind a large tree to catch her breath and rub the area.

God, this was a mess. She should have left Carson the moment Logan finished her surgery. Now, not only was the town in danger, but the man she loved was also risking his life for an outcome that may not exist. Her father wasn't going to rest until she was found and either dead or sold.

Bile rose in her throat as she thought about what Wade had said, that she was going to be sold to a man that wanted a new plaything. It was vile and disgusting, she'd rather take her own life than go through that kind of torture.

And Wade was her half brother? Talk about an unexpected turn of events. She had always wanted a sibling, someone she could help her family care for, but her father had vehemently shot her mother down at every request.

She didn't know Wade well, he was always quiet at the shop unless he was stepping out, but apparently, the apple didn't fall far from the tree. He was set on the same sort of vengeance as her father.

The crack of a branch close by perked Alexis' ears. She had been so lost in thought that she had wasted too much time resting. One of the men could have snuck away to find her, or worse, killed Cliff.

Pushing away from the tree, Alexis made her way back to the narrow path, moving as quickly as she could, but the sense that someone was watching her tugged at something deep within her.

She crested the top of a small hill, only to find a man in black approaching her. Oh no, this wasn't in the plan. They couldn't have known about this path; she had lived here for almost a month and she didn't even know. And the path led to Harlan and Cassidy's property, Alexis could only pray that there was no harm to them.

The man continued to stalk toward her and Alexis spun around, running back down the hill. Veering off the path wasn't the smartest decision, getting lost in the woods was one of her worst fears, but right now, it was the only option facing her. She was stuck and it was just a matter of time before one of the men caught up to her. Alexis wasn't familiar with the woods, causing her to slow her pace. Her eyes darted around, looking for anywhere to hide or take cover.

Off in the distance, Alexis saw another shadow moving through the trees. She was trapped.

Turning around, she smacked into the chest of a solid black mass. The scream bubbled up in her throat but had no chance to break free as the man lifted her in the air and covered her mouth with his hand.

"You've caused quite a bit of trouble for us. The boss is not pleased," the man tsked against her ear. The rough stubble of his beard scratched her face and she tried to buck away but his hold on her waist was too strong.

Carrying her back to the path, he waited for the other men to join him before making his way back toward the lake. This wasn't how it was supposed to happen. How did she get in this entire mess? All because of her existence? She needed answers and it seemed like she would never get them.

As they continued the trek, even though they were outside in the open air, the men's body odor wafted across her nose. She gagged behind her clamped mouth at the scent. Wearing all black in the summer's heat wasn't always the smartest choice.

The opening for the lake came into view and Alexis sighed in relief at the sight of Cliff's back. She had never felt such exaltation during a worse circumstance. The only thing that came close was when Heath found her outside her father's bunker.

Alexis' body grew tighter, if possible, as the elephant of a man carried her closer to their pack.

Suddenly one man fell to the ground and her captor's arm tightened around her waist as he stopped in his tracks. A moment later, another man fell, then a third.

From her perspective, she couldn't make out where the shots were coming from, but knowing Cliff, Alexis assumed that he had rigged up the area as a precaution. She wanted to get her hands on whatever device he was using to set the weapons off.

"Ow," she grunted behind the man's hand as his arms began to dig into her rib cage.

"I need to call the boss. Keep her quiet," elephant man commanded as he roughly handed her over to a smaller, but equally muscled hulk.

Alexis considered using the switch off to break free and scream for everything she's worth, but she hesitated. She had no idea how many of the men were armed. They could easily take her and Cliff out. The odds weren't in their favor. The exchange happened quickly and she didn't even get the opportunity to kick the man in the shins or groin. They tossed her between them already knowing how she planned to fight, like they've done it many times before. And knowing the type of dirty business they run with her father, she's confident they've seen it all before. They're probably some of the same men that took out her team in the bunker. Death and innocence meant little to them. Demons in a black suit.

From the cabin side of the lake, Alexis' eyes widened as another man approached behind Cliff. He moved stealthy, his crouched position masking the sounds of his feet crunching on the ground while Cliff mocked the men standing before him.

A second man followed behind him as the first man lifted a crowbar in the air. As the newcomer buttoned his suit jacket, Alexis recognized him immediately – her father.

Biting her captor's hand, Alexis wrenched her face free and shouted Cliff's name just as the crowbar collided with the back of his head.

"No! Cliff!"

Alexis had been in a panic before, but nothing like this. Nothing like watching a blindsided Cliff helplessly fall to the ground, his lifeless body landing with a thud.

"Cliff!" she cried out again, her heart shredded inside her chest. Her body acted on reflex as grief consumed her. Alexis' legs and arms flailed about uncontrollably. She pushed against the captor's hold, trying to reach the man that held her heart.

Regardless of her fight, she was carried back toward the other side of the lake, her father watching their approach with each step. She felt so much hatred toward the man that she shared DNA with.

"Glad to see you've finally come around," he sneered.

Alexis, still squirming in the captor's hold, leaned her head toward her father's. Without a thought to the consequences, she spit in his face. The moisture landed in his hair and on his tanned skin. She seethed at him, her chest heaving as he reached for a handkerchief and wiped away the wetness.

She was not expecting the left hook after her father delicately placed the cloth back into his pocket. She tasted the blood from her now split lip, the fleshy skin catching on a jeweled gold ring he wore on his index finger.

"You've always been too defiant for your own good. Take her to the car, we're on a tight schedule."

"What do you want us to do with the man?" one of the men asked as the captor carried her past Cliff's limp body lying on the wet ground, the edge of the lake nipping at his legs.

"Toss him in the lake."

A few of the men took turns kicking at Cliff's abdomen, and Alexis winced at every punt.

Wake up, Cliff!

But he didn't hear her internal plea. And as the men shoved his massive body into the dark pool of water, any hope Alexis hung on to disintegrated into the air. He made no movement as his body floated face down in the same place they had skinny-dipped not long ago. She thought she knew of despair, knew of loss, but those thoughts are nothing compared to the hopelessness washing over her.

This couldn't be happening. There had to be a way out.

Knowing that her survival rate nearly became non-existent if they got her in the car, Alexis tried to buy herself more time.

Her luck swayed in her favor as the men carried her back toward the cabin. Just as they rounded the top of the porch movement from the field caught her eye. At first, she thought it was just an animal, but she saw a bright red shirt as the person hurried toward the tree line.

Preston.

She didn't know how the man knew to come or that Cliff needed his help, but she won't look a gift horse in the mouth.

Distracted, she almost missed that they'd opened the back door and were shoving her inside the cabin. Wade's lifeless body was ignored as the men stepped around him.

"Where did he keep his weapons?" her father asked as he began tossing objects around the room, ripping doors off of cabinets, and ripping the couch cushions. She grimaced at the mess that they made to Cliff's home.

"Where?" her father shouted at her when she didn't answer.

Like she was going to give up that information to him.

"I don't know."

Standing nose to nose with her, Lev fumed, spit spraying from his mouth as he spoke. "Don't lie to me, girl."

Remembering her father's phone call at the shop, she used his words for her against him. "I'm not lying. I'm just a dumb whore, remember?"

This time she expected the hit and masked her flinch as his uppercut knocked her teeth against each other.

"Search the house," he commanded his men, except for the captor holding her against his frame. The small elephant man stayed still.

Time. She needed time.

"I don't suppose you'll allow me to change? I'm sure whomever you're taking me to won't appreciate the blood or medical scrubs," she tried to reason with her father using the techniques she developed for interrogations.

"You suppose correctly."

The beast holding her replied, "I don't know, boss. Harposia doesn't like us not looking our best."

Idiot.

"You idiot. Keep your mouth shut." At least she and her father both agreed on something. Shaking his head, her father looked her over, sneering as he took in her ragged appearance. Hell, if he ran through the woods for dear life, he probably wouldn't look too great either. "You have five minutes to change into something sensible. If I were you, I wouldn't consider doing something stupid. And wash your face, you look like a mess."

She tried to cock her eyebrow at him, knowing that he was the reason she looked the way that she did, but the swelling on her face was already hindering her movements.

"Stand guard at the door," her father told his minion, who promptly carried her toward the hallway.

He dropped her at the foot of the door and she barely had a chance to catch herself before she landed on her bottom. As Alexis stepped inside the room, she moved to close the door, but the beast reached out and stopped the motion.

Great. She got an audience too.

Alexis stepped toward the dresser where Cliff allowed her to place her clothes in the drawer. From the full-length mirror in the corner, she could see the man watching her back, but she knew that he couldn't see but a sliver of her. Grabbing a tunic style tank top, Alexis figured she could put this on first, giving her a little bit of coverage as she tugged on a pair of shorts.

Lifting the dirty shirt over her head, her intake of breath was followed by a sharp pain under her ribs, most likely where the man had kept her pinned against him. Biting her cheek to counter the ache, Alexis slipped the bright pink tank over her chest.

Reaching in the second drawer, Alexis moved aside a few pairs of pants in search of her denim shorts. Hopefully, that's what the muscled-man believed she was doing. Below the second pair of pants rested her loaded gun. She didn't need to check it to make sure that it was ready to go. It was small and compact and if she settled it a certain way along the waist of her shorts, it wasn't as noticeable.

Toeing off her shoes, she shimmied the scrub pants over her hips, trying her best to ignore the muscled man's gaze in the mirror as he stared at her ass. Holding the gun and shorts in one hand, she slid her legs through the holes and tugged them up her thighs. A quick tie of her tennis shoes and she was as prepared as she could be.

Right now, the only prayer she had was that her father didn't have her searched. She's counting on his underestimation of her skills.

Alexis moved to exit the room, the security guard crossing his arms as he blocked her in.

"I'm going to the bathroom to wash my face."

He narrows his eyes but allowed her to pass. Her shoulders brushed across his frame and she tried not to cower at the contact. Alexis got the impression that he didn't always agree with her father's command and only did so because Lev was the boss.

"I'd like to use the toilet, please," she tried to ask nicely, hating how the act of pleasantries had her almost swallowing her tongue.

"Make it quick. Your five minutes is almost up," he growled.

Alexis guessed because there was no window in the bathroom that he assumed she couldn't go anywhere. Go - no. Plan - yes. Turning on the sink faucet, Alexis began rummaging through the lower cabinet until she found the small device, no bigger than the palm of her hand. She flipped it open and grabbed one of the small trackers inside. She placed it in the center of her bra, hoping that if worst came to worst, Dylan could use Cliff's computers to track her.

She took the time to rinse her face free of the blood before opening the door to the bathroom. Her father now stood with her guard.

"Your time is up. Time to go."

Muscle man gripped her arm tightly, and she was thankful he didn't grip around her waist again. Once they were back in the living room, the last of the men filed in saying that they found no weapons outside.

She hoped Preston was able to get to Cliff without these men noticing. And if she had any wishes left, she wished that Cliff survived.

Alexis was tugged through the house and as she reached the porch, she gazed at the cabin wistfully in one last goodbye. She'd miss Cliff. This place was their beginning and their end, their love story made out of years of heartache and loneliness.

The group paused at the top of the steps on the porch, something close by startled them.

"Do you smell that?"

Closing her eyes, Alexis let her sense of smell take over.

Gas.

"Smell what?" her father asked the man as he sniffed the air.

The men closest to her began taking heaps of air into their systems, trying to determine the scent. She could hear the raspy sounds of their inhales.

With her eyes still closed another noise pinged, a soft clicking off in the distance. Instantly she knew what that meant and she tried to jerk her arm away, tried to free herself.

"Hey, stop it now," her captor shouted just as the first blast exploded at the back of the cabin.

The group moved collectively as the blasts continued.

"Get the girl in my car," her father shouted, and the beast-man lifted her and ran toward the town car.

Alexis fought against the man as he shoved her into the back seat. She kicked and screamed, but nothing worked. With an elbow to her stomach, Alexis hunched over as he pushed her inside at the same time her father pried open the car door and settled in the seat as if nothing was amiss.

The sound of the doors locking echoed in the car as the muscled man closed the driver's door. He moved the car at lightning speed down the path. Turning in her seat, Alexis watched as Cliff's home went up in a ball of flame and ash. The cloud of smoke was horrific.

Just as they turned the corner leading them back toward the town, Alexis caught something red off in the distance. It was Preston. And he was not alone.

A plastered smile on her lips, Alexis tried to turn back in the seat, but she was met with a cloth across her mouth and nose. Chloroform filled her lungs as she struggled to breathe. Her kicks became less and less violent until she fell limply against the door of the car.

"Didn't think we'd let you off that easily, did you?"

Chapter Nine

"Come on, man," the muffled voice called out to him. The compressions on his chest ached against his tired muscles and bones.

"Alexis needs you."

Oh, Alexis. He tried to save her, tried to do what was best for both of them, but failed miserably. He deserved to die in the pool of water where they spent their nights to escape the grueling heat.

A bright light beckoned him just beyond his reach, he stretched out toward it, but his arms didn't move.

"Cliff! Come on!" the voice called out again. It seems familiar, but he couldn't pinpoint it. Air swirled in his lungs and an ache pounded at the back of his head. Suddenly water rushed out of his diaphragm and lungs until it was spilling from his mouth.

Cliff coughed uncontrollably as he fought the pull to continue retching up the freshwater.

"Thank goodness," that familiar voice sighed. Preston. Cliff watched as the man sat back on his heels, his own chest heaved with exertion.

The entire afternoon roared to life in Cliff's mind and though he fought off death only seconds ago, his body yearned to move, yearned to fight.

"Alexis," he groaned as he rolled onto all fours. "They have her." Even to his own ears, his voice sounded foreign.

"I know. Look, we need to get out of here. I smell gas."

Oh, shit. The self-destruct. In a last-ditch effort, Cliff set off the self-destruct button from his phone hoping to create a diversion. If the smell of gas had already reached the lake area, then there wasn't much time to waste. The entire process took about ten minutes.

"Can you walk?" Preston asked as he helped Cliff get to his feet. He was unsteady but moved as quickly as possible through the trees.

"How did you find me?"

"Ryker. He called me after you left and said something didn't sit right. Then he saw the black cars barreling down Main Street and kept me in the loop. I'm sorry I didn't get here sooner."

"I'm glad you're here at all," Cliff acknowledged as the field came into view. His muscles continued to shake as they hobbled out of the tree line, just as the rest of his house went up in flames.

"Oh, fuck," Preston shouted, trying to shield his face while Cliff kept his gaze trained on the car speeding away. Once it was out of sight, Cliff looked back to find his truck just at the edge of the dancing flames.

Grabbing Preston's arm, he asked, "I need you to take me to my apartment above the studio. And I need you to get Joseph to put this flame out before it gets too bad."

Typing on his phone, Preston nodded until they reached his cruiser hidden behind the brush along the gravel path.

No sooner than the cruiser pulled into the back of his shop did the town descend on him. Many offering their worries for Alexis, others comforting him.

This large extended family wanted nothing more than for him to get Alexis home safe and sound. It was his own wish.

Harlan guided everyone into Cliff's shop while he, Preston, and Dylan made their way upstairs. Dylan showed up with the rest of the town.

"Hey, man, I'm sorry," Ryker apologized as if the entire fiasco was on his hands, but Cliff assured him that her father and half brother fooled them all. Cliff went on to explain how Wade had been in it. He came to town at first to learn about his sister, knowing that she had been here a few years back. The side missions are in her FBI file. But when her father put a bounty on her, he wanted to be the one to bring her in.

"Fucking, sicko. Both of them," Dylan growled. "Selling your own daughter and sister into sex trafficking. I just can't fathom it."

"They think women are weak. If Alexis has her wits about her, I'm sure she's giving them hell right now," Cliff told them as he sat at the large computer in the center of the room, bringing up the tracking application.

"I placed a tracker in her shoes when she came to live with me. Let's hope that it's still working and didn't get knocked loose. Or that the stubborn woman found it and took it out."

Clicking on a few keys, a map came to life on the screen with two small dots, one right on top of the other.

"God, I love that woman."

"What?" Preston asked, leaning closer to the monitor.

"Somehow, she found my box of trackers, which doesn't surprise me, the little snoop. But she placed one on her body. So now we have two trackers to follow."

"Smart girl."

"Preston, did you get my message relayed?"

His friend nodded and explained that he called the Asheville department and they were setting up a police barricade, but they needed a time frame. With the tracking system, they would be able to stop them before Lev had a chance to get to the larger city.

"How did they get through Main Street without anyone seeing them?" Cliff asked Ryker.

"From what I can tell, they took the service roads. They never showed on the cameras."

"Fucking, Wade. He probably scoped out all of the possible exits to the town. God, I'm a fool," Cliff admonished himself.

"No, you're not. I ran the background check for you, remember?" Preston pointed out. "He was clear, only a speeding ticket on his record. Now that I know it is her half brother, I can see the resemblance. Surprised none of us saw it before."

Dylan's phone began to ping with incoming messages and he relayed to the group that most of the men downstairs were heading to Cliff's cabin to help put out the fire.

The sound of a knock on the apartment door had the men spinning on their feet and leaving the secret room, guns pulled ready to fire. All except Cliff who lost his at the lake. Cliff took a look at the small monitor by the door. Something about the man was familiar and as the stranger looked around Cliff pressed the button to open the apartment door.

The man's eyes widened in surprise as he turned to find Preston, Dylan, and Ryker standing with weapons drawn, but then his bright green eyes settled on Cliff.

"Hey. . . ugh. . . I thought that maybe I could help."

"You're the new bar owner."

"I am. I heard about what's happening while I was walking home and thought that maybe I could help somehow."

Cliff narrowed his eyes at the stranger, but then realized the man without any friends in town was offering to help him get his woman back.

Holding out his hand, Cliff greeted the man. "Thanks. I'll take anything I can get. I'm Cliff. What's your plan?"

Returning his shake, the stranger replied, "Landon. And do you have access to a CB radio?"

Preston nodded and flew out of the apartment toward the police station a block away.

Cliff explained to Landon what they were looking at and the four men kept their eyes trained on the tracking system, watching as the car began to approach the service road's entrance to the main highway.

"You a spy?" Landon asked, breaking the silence.

Cliff shook his head, though truthfully, it was probably the closest designation for his job that he could fathom. "You going to tell us anything about yourself?"

"Not today."

"What made you come out of hiding today?"

"I've spent enough time in a shell, figured it was as good a time as any."

True enough. Cliff could understand, he was the same way at one time.

Two minutes later, Preston rushed back into the room, sweat lining his brow, but he was barely out of breath as he handed over the CB radio and all of its parts.

Landon worked at setting it up as he explained that they'll try channel nineteen first since it was the most common.

"Tell me again what the plan is?" Preston asked wearily.

"We're going to ask for some assistance. Believe me, when those truckers hear that there is a kidnapping, they're going to shut down that highway faster than you can say freeze."

Flipping a switch, a low humming sound filled the room.

Landon brought the mic to his mouth.

"This is Irish Whiskey asking for help."

At first, there was no response, then the room filled with a dozen or so confirmations.

"We've got a kidnapping at your backdoor on 40. Need a convoy and stop."

Rogers and ten-fours answered in response.

Landon gave the description of the black town car and its current location before ending the transmission.

"All right. You guys stay here. Preston and I are going behind them."

"I'm coming too. We need to turn these guys into the FBI," Dylan explained.

"Good luck," Landon said as he left. Ryker turned back to the monitor, promising to keep them in the loop if anything changed.

***

Her body jostled against the seat and Alexis was taken back to the moment she was lying in the backseat of Heath's stolen car, barely clinging to life. The car dipped and her head cracked against the door, the pain sending stars behind her closed eyes. Unable to open her mouth, her moan rumbled in her chest.

Her eyes shot open in alarm only to find her mouth duct-taped closed and her arms tied behind her with plastic ties.

"Mmm!" she screamed behind the tape, flailing her legs, which were also duct-taped together at the ankles. "Mmm!"

"Calm down. Don't want you hurting yourself. Had to take precautions. Couldn't have you going after me with that gun you tucked into your waistband." Her eyebrows rose in surprise. How could he have figured that out? "You may have fooled the brawn, but you can't fool the brains," her father snarled. Alexis looked up at the rearview mirror, meeting the narrowed gaze of the muscled driver who had stood outside the bedroom door.

Alexis surmised that they were on the outskirts of town on an old back road. She couldn't have been out of it too long, thirty minutes tops. When she had helped locate Sydney, Alexis had memorized these paths on the map, knowing that they all led to a service entrance of Highway 40.

It was another five minutes before the weaving gravel path gave way to the opening of the main road. The driver pulled the car onto the shoulder and merged into an opening in traffic. They were heading toward Asheville, and if Alexis suspected correctly, to the airport to hitch a ride on a chartered plane. She needed to come up with something fast. Some way to deter the men from getting her on a flight. But what could she do without the ability to speak?

She felt like The Little Mermaid without the happily ever after in her future.

Her aggravation grew as the car zipped and zagged around the slower vehicles, everyone moving out of the way as if the town car was carrying someone of importance. Frustration built and bloomed inside her body, festering under her skin like molten lava ready to explode.

The driver honked the horn as a trucker in the left lane refused to move over despite his lower speed. Beside their car, another trucker pulled up alongside them, and another in the rear. Alexis dared to peek out of her window, silently begging the driver beside them to take notice.

"Yes!" she cried behind the tape as the driver winked down at her then sped up his truck to run beside the leader. She didn't know how or why, but somehow, they were going to help her. Cliff and Preston must have got word out to them.

Her survival instincts kicked in at the knowledge that she wasn't alone, that they were all fighting with her.

With renewed spirit Alexis, brought her knees to her chest, twisted in her seat, and kicked at her father's face. Over and over again, she jerked her legs back and forth, ramming his head against the window.

Victory was short-lived as a lower kick fell at her father's shoulder, allowing him the chance to grip her ankles and twist, sending her falling face first onto the floor. Alexis tried to get up onto her knees but her father slammed his feet onto the middle of her back and behind her knees.

RENEE HARLESS

The pain was excruciating as stars danced behind her eyes.

Her moan went unheard as the driver began to swerve the car.

"What do you want me to do, Boss? They're saying it is stopped up ahead."

Faintly in the background, Alexis could hear the guide on the navigation system speaking.

"No more exits for another five miles."

"Are there any side roads to go around?"

"Not unless you want me to drive in a field."

"Do it."

Alexis braced against the floor, her father's feet pressed against her back, as she prepped for the jostle of the car to veer off the highway.

Instead, she was met with the thunderous sound of tractor-trailer trucks braking beside the car.

"Oh, shit," the driver cried out as the car spun. Alexis closed her eyes and tucked her head as close as possible against her chest when the first impact landed on her father's side of the car, the next on hers. A weightless sensation floated through her until she realized that the vehicle was airborne.

Without a seatbelt or any way to hold herself down, Alexis feared for the first time that she may not survive.

The car flipped over the hood deploying the airbags with a pop and then settled upside down, the car spinning slightly on the roof. The only thing holding her in place was her father's foot on the back of her knees and the way her head lodged under the front passenger seat.

She wondered if her father survived the impact and the muscled man driving the car.

"Get me out of here, now," her father shouted, finally releasing his foot from her knees.

It happened slowly. First, her feet descended toward the ground, which was now the roof of the car, and then her head began to slip from its cubby under the seat. With no way to brace for the fall, Alexis' shoulder took the full impact. The same shoulder that took the bullet.

A muffled groan cried from behind the tape over her mouth. Wetness pooled against her lower lids as her head collided against the metal.

From her position on the ground, she watched as the driver pushed aside the deployed airbag and wrenched his door open. Unleashing his seatbelt, he toppled forward but pulled himself upright as he moved out of the car. He spared no backward glance at his boss, or her. He took off on foot toward the woods.

Jerking her head in the other direction, she witnessed the aftermath of their collision, pileups of cars as far as the eye could see. The truck drivers began to step out of their vehicles, a few with weapons of their own raised toward her father's car.

"You think that they're here to save you?" her father's voice drew her attention and she watched in horror as he took her own gun and maneuvered out of the vehicle, gripping her feet to pull her with him. No amount of wiggling would set her free.

Just as his son had done earlier, Lev stood with one arm wrapped tightly around her and the other with a gun pointed to her head. She had to give him credit for being smart enough to have her facing him. Had she been turned around, she would have bucked against him.

"Back up!" he yelled to the truckers as he took a step away from his car, having to drag her with him due to her taped ankles. She could already decipher his plan as his eyes darted around; with her as a hostage, he was going to steal one of the trucks to make his escape.

She really hoped that it didn't come to that.

The truckers backed away, but never dropped their weapons. As he pulled her between the two trucks that blocked the highway, her view of the men drifted away.

"You're a bigger pain now than you were as a child. Look what you're making me do. You couldn't just come without a fight. Pain in my ass, just like your mother."

He dragged her a few more yards until he reached the driver's door of one of the vehicles. Pressing her against the metal of the truck, he pried the door open with the arm that had been wrapped around her waist, then pushed her up and inside the truck.

Alexis tried to fight. God, she gave it everything she had. Kicking, twisting, falling, but to no avail. He managed to get her inside and pushed her over until he was able to get inside himself, gun positioned at her the entire time.

Turning the key in the ignition, Lev moved to shut the door, only to find himself with a gun positioned at his head.

"Drop the weapon. Get out of the vehicle now with your hands up or so help me. I will blow your head into a million little pieces."

Alexis cried behind the tape. Preston stood at the ready with his gun drawn at Lev as Cliff stood beside him, with his eyes trained on her.

"Think you two scare me," her father said, trying again to pull the door closed.

Before she knew what was happening her father's scream filled the cab of the truck, followed by the clanging of his gun onto the floor.

"You shot my hand!"

"You took too long. Resisting arrest. Now get out of the vehicle with your hands up," Preston bellowed.

Her father stalled, his hand held tightly against his chest. She could tell he was weighing his options as he looked back and forth between the wheel and Preston.

Alexis was tired of waiting. Pulling her knees to her chest once more, she kicked at her father until he fell from the truck, his face landing on the hot asphalt. Preston immediately got to work cuffing Lev while he screamed that he wanted to go to the hospital.

Cliff didn't watch. He launched himself inside the truck and pulled her to him. Even restrained she could feel his embrace wrap around her completely.

"Oh, sweetheart." She was amazed to see the moisture filling in his eyes, his love for her evident in each tear. "This is going to hurt," he told her, placing his fingers at the edge of the tape. She nodded and he pulled the strip. Her skin felt like it had been pulled off and she cried out in agony, Alexis's body pulling away with each removal.

"I'm so sorry," his voice was choked up as he lifted her ankles and repeated the motion, the sensitive skin throbbing afterward.

Hating to turn away from him, she did so to show him her wrists cuffed with plastic ties. Using a pocket knife dangling from the rearview mirror, he sliced through the thick plastic and set her free. Cliff didn't have a chance to hang the knife back in place before she launched herself at him.

"You came for me!"

He wrapped her in his arms so tightly that she could barely take a breath, it was the best thing she had ever felt.

"Of course I did, I love you."

"I love you too," she cried.

"Sorry, guys. The ambulance is here." Alexis recognized the voice as Dylan's.

Pulling back, Cliff only adjusted his hands toward her face and placed the most gentle kiss on her lips. She would melt into a puddle at his feet if they weren't in this particular situation, the kiss was that sweet and potent.

Stepping out of the vehicle, Cliff lifted Alexis into his arms and carried her tenderly down the same path that her father had dragged her through in his means to escape.

"Did you catch the man that fled?" Cliff asked Dylan who walked behind them.

"They have the dogs on him," he said. At first, Alexis didn't know what he meant, but then she saw the Asheville police SUVs with K-9 unit emblazoned along the side.

As they reached the ends of the truck a round of applause sounded. It began softly, just one or two people, then the noise became a thunderous pulse. Alexis rested her head on Cliff's shoulder as they made their way through the crowd. Some of the truckers patted Cliff on the back; others sobbed in their happiness of her escape. The emotions were overwhelming and exhaustion tugged at Alexis.

"Sleep, sweetheart. I'll be right by your side."

As he laid her on the stretcher, he followed the EMTs into the back of the ambulance.

The paramedic wrapped a blood pressure cuff around her bicep and the other attached a pulse monitor on the tip of her finger.

"Hey, Cliff," she whispered, turning her head away from the machines to face him. His clothes were covered in mud and dust, his face still a slight shade of gray from where he must have fought death and won.

"Yeah," he replied, reaching over to take her free hand in his.

"You never did tell me your real name."

She cracked a smile as he chuckled. "You're right, I didn't. My real name is Michael."

Closing her eyes, Alexis let the desire to sleep overtake her, but not before mumbling, "Michael, my angel and protector."

Chapter Ten

The pounding of the hammer in his hand vibrated against the newly formed calluses on his palm. The ache was bittersweet. He could use the air compressed nail gun to set the boards for the frame of the living room, but he enjoyed the feel of the tool in his hand.

"We'd be done by now if you would use a power tool," Austin complained, the rest of the Connelly men joining with a few chuckled as they helped him finish framing the inside of his new cabin.

Well, it wasn't going to be a cabin any longer. Once Cliff was cleared to build on the land, he and Austin drew up the plans for a proper mountain lodge.

It was going to be everything he had ever dreamed of. But one thing was missing.

It had been over a month since he heard from Alexis and his heart stung whenever he thought about her or was reminded of her. And here on his property, everything reminded him of Alexis. He lived in a perpetual state of heartbreak, moping around the town no matter how many times Amy tried to cheer him up. Somehow the woman found out his love of Butterfinger candy bars and he'd found bouquets of them at his shop every day since he returned to Carson.

Cliff's phone buzzed in his back pocket and he set down the hammer on the workbench and fished it out.

"Finally, maybe now I can get the drywall up," Austin mumbled as he took over nailing the board in place that Cliff had been working on.

Cliff couldn't hold back his look of disappointment at the image of the familiar truck cruising down his driveway.

He prayed every night that Alexis came back to him, even knowing that her return wasn't something she could control. The moment she had been admitted to the hospital, the FBI had swarmed the building and forcefully shoved him away. He barely got to say goodbye to her before he was kicked out and told that everything was now part of a criminal investigation.

He had been treated like a second-class citizen when he probably had a higher clearance than most of the men and women in Alexis' room. His only consolation was that Heath had returned and was by her side. He messaged Cliff daily to keep him in the loop, Cliff only wondered why Alexis couldn't do the same.

"Are we ready for walls?" Cliff asked as he shoved his phone back in his pocket and turned toward the three men in the same room. The rest had ventured upstairs to finish the framing.

"Can we take a break? It's fucking hot as hell in here." Logan leaned against the wall that would be the foyer, sweat dripping down his face.

It was hot. The middle of summer in Carson could be brutal on an average day, but they had extreme temperatures for a week now. Luckily, the HVAC system was scheduled to be installed the next day.

"Yeah, we can wait until it starts to cool off."

A thud on the porch brought everyone's attention toward the front door. Landon stood sheepishly with a cooler at his feet.

With a shrug, he said, "I brought beer."

Though the man remained silent most of the time, Cliff had tried his hardest to include the newcomer. From what he learned so far, the bar Landon had been spending his time renovating was slated to open in early fall, right at the height of the beer season. He'd been asking their advice on the best local breweries to include on tap.

"Beer!" the collective group shouted as they pound down the steps and through the front door, every person reaching into the cooler with thanks to Landon. Cliff watched as the group settled and relaxed on the porch they'd helped build.

After the explosion on his property, the fire had raged for several hours, destroying most of the woods behind his cabin. He had felt terrible about the destruction, still did. And now, as he looked around the burnt crisps of trees that succumbed to the fire, his chest twinged. He felt as dead as those branches.

The only bright spot from the devastation was the cool breeze off the lake. Being in the nook of the valley the space received a constant gentle wind, and with the water, it kept the property cool.

"Man, this place is going to be great when it was done," Harlan claimed as he took a swig of his beer. "I may get Austin to renovate my house while I'm out on tour."

"You're going on tour again? "Austin asked. Cliff was surprised that he seemed to be the only one that knew that secret.

"Yeah, but this time Cassidy is coming along. It's just a for few weeks."

"Just let me knew what you're thinking and I can get it drawn up. Summer is the busy season, but I can get a team ready. No worries."

"Thanks, brother."

The men finish their breaks, and head back inside, groaning as they grabbed sheets of drywall in groups of two. They started with the upstairs, working their way from one end of the house to the other, finishing the four bedrooms before the sun began setting beyond the mountains.

Cliff walked with the men outside, waving as they left for the evening, all of them promising to return the next day to complete their work. He's grateful for their help, most of them taking time away from their jobs to help him. They understand his urgency. He wasn't finishing it for himself; he was rushing it in the hopes that Alexis returned.

The night crept in, setting the cabin in a familiar navy blanket, only the light from the outdoor porch light illuminating the space. He sat in the far corner of the porch; his back pressed against the railing as a beer dangled from his hand.

Cliff ignored the sound and the lights of a car as it moved slowly down the path leading to his home. He recognized the engine sound without having to look at the image of the vehicle on his security camera.

"Help yourself to a beer. Landon left the cooler," Cliff called out to Dylan as the man stepped from his truck.

"Thanks. Don't mind if I do. Can Sydney have one too?"

That got his attention. None of the Connelly women had made it out this way yet since they started construction. He assumed most of them are probably waiting to get to the decorating part so they could kick him out and do it themselves.

"Sure, have a seat. Though all I can offer is the floor of the porch."

Sydney moved toward him first, Dylan came up the rear grabbing two bottles of beer along the way.

"How are you doing?" Sydney's melodic voice asked as she perched beside him.

"I'm good. Wish the house was coming along faster, but most of that's my own doing."

"You can't rush these things," she pointed out with a gentle tap to his arm before taking the beer from her husband. Cliff got the slightest suspicion that she wasn't referring to the house.

"Amy got the kids?" Cliff asked, knowing that Amy watched a set of grandkids every night. That woman was the epitome of a grandma.

"That she does. We were on our way home from dinner and wanted to stop by. I hadn't seen the place yet."

Taking a sip of beer, Cliff added, "Not much to look at."

"But it will be beautiful when it is done."

The trio sat in silence for a few minutes, the sound of bugs moving toward the light and zipping away played a symphony of music with the crickets and frogs.

"I hear you were given another mission."

Cliff knew not to question how Dylan got his intel, it was about as secret as receiving his own. And it was the truth. He got the call two days ago, but this one would take him overseas for a little less than a year.

"Yep."

"Also, hear you haven't responded yet."

"Also, correct."

The softness of a woman's touch brushed against his arm and Cliff looked down to find Sydney's hand settled there. Her pale skin a stark contrast to his dark and colorful tattoos; even in the darkness, the difference was jarring.

"You miss her. It's okay to admit it. No one will think any less of you."

After a deep exhale, Cliff confessed, "I do."

"I know it was terrible what happened, and I couldn't believe they wouldn't let you stay with her at the hospital. I would have been devastated if that happened with Dylan. But trust that she loves and misses you too."

"It has been over a month." Putting his fear into words was like a knife through his chest, spearing and twisting with every letter.

"Don't give up on her yet, Cliff."

What more could he do? With every frame and wall he added to this house, this house where he dreamt of making a family with her, it was as if he was hammering the nails to his own coffin. Every day without her was one more day of losing himself.

He remembered the pain after his ex-wife died, how he had felt that he was the reason for her death. But this agony of not having Alexis was ten-times worse because he loved her with everything that he was.

"Thanks for stopping by guys. I have an early morning," he fibbed. He'd be up early, but that was because he'd spend the night counting down every minute in the hopes that he'd see her again.

Cliff watched as Dylan and Sydney drove away then headed inside the cabin. He set up one of the upstairs rooms as his makeshift bedroom. It was the smallest in the house. He couldn't bear to make the largest bedroom his room yet, even with the blank walls, all he saw was her.

The air was hot and muggy, just as it had been those nights he and Alexis opted to take a swim in the lake as a reprieve from the heat. Cliff plugged in a box fan and opened the windows, letting the warm breeze run over his skin. Lying just under the window, Cliff tilted his head back and counted the stars, making it to about thirty-two thousand before the sun broke through the sky. It was not the first time he's stayed up the entire night, nor would it be his last.

The relief of the new HVAC system being installed was immediate. The Connelly men were equally as gracious, helping to finish hanging the drywall throughout the house while the servicemen worked on adding the air vents.

"I ordered dinner from Angie's as a thank you," Cliff told the group of men nailing in the last ceiling sheetrock.

"Damn, you're my new best friend," Brooks joked as he shoved Logan aside to perch over one of the blowing air vents. The HVAC had only been running for about two hours, so the air in the house was still warm, but it was cooling rapidly.

Cliff's phone alerted him of an incoming vehicle and he told the men that the food was here. A gentle knock on the door sounded and Cliff opened it wide expecting to come face to face with a teenager holding various take out bags, only to stand slack-jawed at a recreation of his photo of Alexis.

"What the-" his question died off as the photo lowered, only to reveal the woman in question holding the image.

"I'm sorry it took me so long to get here."

Fuck, she looked gorgeous. Her shorter hair tucked neatly behind her ears, and her FBI issued blue shirt and black pants were gone, replaced by a tight black T-shirt and jean shorts.

"Are you really here?" Cliff's voice cracked from the hoarseness. He had imagined her pulling up to his cabin so many times, but somehow his imagination hadn't done her any justice.

"I'm really here, to stay, if you'd let me."

God this woman. Let her? He planned to never let her go again.

Reaching out he pulled her by the back of her head and crushed their lips together, not even the corner of the canvas digging into his abdomen discouraged him from staking his claim. She returned his kiss as eagerly, as if she'd been craving it just as much.

A cough sounded behind Alexis and Cliff and he pulled his lips away, anger spewing at the cause of the interruption. The pimply adolescent held up the plastic bags from Angie's, silently pleading that Cliff spare him his life.

"We'll just take these inside. You two go. . .catch up," Dylan explained as he took the bags from the delivery driver and marched them inside, winking at Cliff's surprise guest along the way.

Alexis took a small step back, Cliff's hand falling back down by his side as she moved the canvas over to rest on the porch railing.

He could tell she was weighing her words carefully, and after one deep breath she dropped the bomb on him.

"Cliff, I have something I need to tell you."

***

This place was majestic. She stared at the new construction for a solid minute before she got the strength to take the journey up the stairs. Questions bombarded her mind in quick succession. Had she been gone too long? Did he move on? Did he move away? Had he missed her?

None of those answers mattered though when he opened the door and pulled her toward him. His mouth sealed against hers, taking every ounce of love she possessed for him. He held her head so tightly he seemed to think she would slip away at any moment.

Even now, as they walked toward the lake, he kept glancing her way, as if she'd slip away at any moment. He guided her to the end of the dock, the same place they had sat when she stayed with him that first day.

"The mission I was sent on, the one that brought me here, isn't over." Cliff stiffened beside her as he digested her words. "But," she added, laying a hand on his arm, "I won't be a part of the team."

"What does that mean?"

"Well, plainly it means that I quit. But you know with any mission, you can't just quit. I had to go through days of debriefing and interrogations. I also had to sit in and listen to my father's depositions. The days turned into weeks, and those weeks turned into a month."

The time away from him had been agony. When she was finally cleared to leave her position, she was unsure of herself for the first time. Alexis packed up her apartment, left a note for her landlord, and rented a car. She drove through the night to get back to Carson, to get to Cliff. She had been away long enough.

But as he stared across the water, Alexis worried that the time had been too long.

"So, what happens with the investigation on the cartel and sex trafficking?"

"Heath will take it over. He should have been the leader to begin with. Harposia is still running it from her jail cell, though no one had figured out how, nor do I think they ever will. My father's second in command has moved up the ranks."

"The threat against you still exists."

"Maybe, maybe not."

This was the part she hadn't figured out how to disclose. With the help of the FBI and the hospital staff, Alexis pretty much wiped herself off the face of the earth. The doctors forged her chart and said she didn't survive after the brain trauma of the accident. Cliff nodded as she explained everything as detailed as she could. Many of the parts she wasn't sure of herself. Somehow strings were pulled and she was provided with a new last name, social security card, and passport.

"What's the name?" Cliff asked, reaching over to take her hand in his.

"Walker. I asked for the last name Walker." Walker was a common last name, and at the time, she had but a moment to decide. It was the first thing that came to mind.

"You have my last name," Cliff whispered, his thumb stroking back and forth along her knuckles as he stared at their joined hands.

"I didn't mean to be presumptuous. I can go have it changed."

"You will not," he growled. The pad of his thumb stopped over her ring finger. "It just made this part easier."

"What part?"

"Alexis Walker. Will you marry me? I've been in misery without you."

"Yes. For the rest of my days, yes."

The morning sun gleamed on Alexis' back, warming her already heated skin. The heavy arm of a tattooed man rested along her shoulders, keeping her close.

A smile broke on her lips as she remembered how he kicked his friends out of his home and made love to her for hours upon hours last night. Her bones and muscles still ached in the best possible way.

"Good morning, beautiful," Cliff's deep voice said as he turned her body to face him, kissing her along the corner of her mouth.

"Morning. What's on the agenda today?" she asked, though she wasn't opposed to spending the day in bed with him making up for lost time.

"Well, I have a shop to run, but first I'm thinking a quick trip to the jewelry store and breakfast at Angie's."

"Shouldn't we do breakfast first?"

"If I've learned anything in this town, it's that if you can kill two birds with one stone then throw it into a flock."

"I don't know what that means," she laughed.

"I think Amy is rubbing off on me. It just means if you wear your engagement ring to breakfast then more people can confirm the gossip."

"Which means, less people bothering you."

"Exactly."

"You're such a hermit."

"But you love me anyway."

"I do. I really do."

Getting dressed took three times longer as it should. Cliff tugged away every article of clothing that she put on until he had her back in her naked state and showed her again how much he loved her. Thoroughly and numerous times.

By the time they made it to Angie's, the diner was already serving lunch. It only took a few seconds before Shirley and Temple Fitzgerald of the Lady Busy Bees noticed her arrival, and then their gazes fell on the three-carat marquise diamond resting on her ring finger.

Congratulations followed them through the town as they walked to Cliff's shop. She waved at people she'd never seen before, but unlike last time, the unfamiliar faces didn't frighten her.

"I'm going to run across the street real quick. I'll be right back." She kissed Cliff's cheek then made her way over to the Carson Police station.

Inside she found a young woman chewing loudly on a piece of gum, while the phone rang continuously. Alexis stopped just inside the room, waiting for the woman to take the call, not wanting to interrupt. But the woman just stared at her as if she'd grown two heads.

"I'm sorry, are you going to get that?" Alexis
asked.

"No, I'm on a break."

Wow, okay. Let's hope that wasn't an
emergency.

"Is Preston he-"

"Zia, if I'm paying you through your lunch then
you need to answer the phone. And stop having your
boyfriends call this line. It is for emergencies."

The woman simply shrugged then picked up the
next ringing line.

Alexis called out his name as he steered himself
back toward the offices.

"Alexis, welcome back. What can I do for you?"

"Do you have a minute? I wanted to talk to you
about something."

Twenty minutes later Alexis left the station with
a new pep in her step and she couldn't wait to give Cliff
the good news. She had been afraid that Preston
wouldn't be open to someone encroaching on his
territory, but she was pleasantly surprised when he
asked when she could start. He begged for that day to
be tomorrow.

"Cliff," she shouted as she walked into the shop,
smiling at a quiet girl with cute black rimmed glasses
perched on her nose. She was manning the desk like
Alexis had when she worked at the shop.

"Back here," he called out. As she turned the corner, instead of finding him drawing or working on a client, he was toying with a camera in his hands.

"Is that your camera?"

"It sure is. I haven't used it in quite a while. Now that I've pulled back on some of my government work, I thought I'd get back into it."

"No more secret missions?" she asked, thrilled that he's stepping back from the danger. She had heard from Dylan the night before that a new assignment had requested him.

"No more. I turned down the last one offered. Did you get what you needed?"

Alexis gleefully jumped on his lap and explained her new position with Preston as Deputy Sherriff.

"So, you're making Carson home?" Cliff said.

Wrapping her arms around Cliff's neck, she brushed her lips against his, adoring the way he responded to her touch.

"You're my home, Cliff. Wherever you are is home."

Epilogue

"Wow, this is more beautiful than I expected," Alexis whispered as they looked out across the Smoky Mountains from their cabin's balcony.

"Can't argue with that."

Cliff stood a couple feet behind Alexis, mesmerized by her bare back as the ivory slip dress blew in the breeze. With the sun setting just beyond the mountains, the combination of her and the view was breathtaking.

Lifting his camera to his eye, Cliff adjusted the lens and snapped a few pictures. No better way to capture their wedding day than with a few personal pictures.

He had convinced Alexis to take a short trip to Gatlinburg, Tennessee, while Austin put the final touches on Cliff's house in Carson.

Once they arrived, Alexis had immediately asked if he wanted to elope. Like he would turn down making her his wife sooner rather than later.

They grabbed a marriage license at the courthouse and were married in a small chapel the next day. Neither one of them came from large families, it was perfect for Cliff and Alexis. Though Cliff suspected that Mrs. Connelly won't be too keen on not having another wedding to plan.

The sound of the shutters alerted Alexis and she turned on her bare feet, leaning against the railing.

"What are you doing?"

"Capturing something beautiful," he explained as he snapped another picture of her.

"Come here, husband of mine," she beckoned. He couldn't turn her down. "I want one of us together."

Cliff moved to join her against the railing and held up the camera, centering them with the viewfinder. He snapped a few images then placed the camera on an outside table before pulling Alexis to rest against him, wedging her body between him and the railing.

"Thank you, Alexis. For being with me, for loving me. I can't believe I get to call you mine."

"Oh, Cliff," Alexis replied, stroking her fingers against his cheek. "I love you so much. You're everything I ever wanted."

Cliff kissed her slowly, retracing all the grooves in her mouth as if he'd never felt them before. Reaching for her shoulder, Cliff grazed his fingers along the scar left from her bullet wound before tugging the strap of her dress down her arm.

"Why don't we move this inside and I can show you all of the ways I want to love?"

"I was wondering what was taking you so long," she joked as she stepped around him, slipping the other strap down her body. Just as Alexis stepped beyond the threshold of the mountain cabin, her dress pooled at her feet.

"Fuck," Cliff cursed, quickly following her inside.

She was going tempt and tease him every day of his life, and he couldn't wait.

***

He didn't know how she got the consistency perfect, but somehow Sydney made the most delicious, melt in your mouth, donuts he'd ever had.

And Preston didn't even like donuts, despite the fact that cops and donuts went together like peanut butter and jelly. They'd never been his thing.

He sat at the small table watching the woman he had planned to spend his life with add more cupcakes to her display. He screwed that up, just like he had everything else in his life.

Thankfully his feelings for Sydney waned and he saw her as nothing more than a friend. Otherwise, things would be very awkward as his best friend, and Sydney's husband, took the seat across from him.

"Hey, man," Dylan greeted, his The Grill apron still tied around his chest. Preston could barely manage working as the town sheriff and a few missions with his old FBI team when things got slow. He had no idea how Dylan was able to manage his diner, the extra missions he took, and his family.

"Hey," Preston greeted, taking the final bite of donut.

"I asked Alexis and Cliff to join us for lunch, if that's okay."

"Yeah, sure."

It would mean that no one was taking calls at the station, but they'd manage. Since Alexis' case was closed two months ago everything had died down some.

A few minutes later, Cliff and Alexis join them, their smiles lighting up the room as they stepped inside. Preston was happy for them both; they deserved it about as much as anyone he knew.

And by the way Alexis kept a firm grip on her husband's backside, Preston was positive that kids wouldn't be far behind their wedding.

Marriage and family didn't seem to be in the cards for him, but much to his mother's dismay, he was fine with bachelorhood. Though Carson was small it was not hard to find a woman to warm his bed at night.

They ordered lunch, a few sandwiches and chips, and Dylan told them that his "other" boss would like to see if they were interested in working with the local FBI as needed.

As Preston expected Cliff and Alexis declined, but he agreed to learn more. It was not that he needed the money, but rather he was interested in finding something to occupy his time.

"So, when is the big day?" Dylan asked Alexis, though Preston already knew. He was probably one of the few.

"Well, it already passed. We eloped over the weekend."

"What?" Sydney shouted from her station.

"I told you," Preston muttered under his breath.

"It was just the right time. And we wanted to get started trying to have a baby."

"Well, what are you doing still working? Shouldn't you be on a honeymoon?" Dylan narrowed his gaze toward Preston, as if he made that decision. He raised his hands in the air in innocence.

"Don't look at me. I tried to pay for a trip to the Caribbean; you know how stubborn she is."

"Hey! I'm right here. And we are going to wait until the season slows so that Cliff can close his shop."

"And what if you're pregnant," Dylan asked, the same question on Preston's lips.

"Oh," she exclaimed looking at her husband. "I hadn't thought about that."

"It's fine. We'll stay close by," Cliff told her, leaning in to place a soft kiss on her lips.

Preston would never lead on that watching his friends fall in love had been like a knife thrusting in his chest repeatedly. He thought one day he'd have that, but that dream was washed away by his own doing.

Finishing their lunches, his friends at the table dispersed, leaving him to catch up on the national news with the paper. Though Alexis' case had been closed, he kept a close eye on any missing girl and drug trafficking cases. The FBI hadn't been able to take out her father's cartel, just put a kink in it.

"Cassidy!" Sydney shouted. "I thought you were on tour with Harlan?"

"I am, we're just passing through. But guess who finally decided to pack her bags and move here?"

"Who?"

Yes, who? Preston wondered, his attention pulled away from the paper and now focused on Cassidy.

"Shelly. I need help finding her a place to stay. She's showing up tomorrow."

Oh no. If there was one woman capable of unraveling him it was that woman. She was smart, beautiful, and had a mouth like a sailor. He had been drawn to her the few times that she had visited.

He couldn't stop the words before they rolled out of his mouth.

"I can help."

Stay in Touch

Newsletter: http://bit.ly/2WokAjS
Author Page: www.facebook.com/authorreneeharless
Reader Group: http://bit.ly/31AGa3B
Instagram: www.instagram.com/renee_harless
Bookbub: www.bookbub.com/authors/renee-harless
Goodreads: http://bit.ly/2TDagOn
Amazon: http://bit.ly/2WsHhPq
Website: www.reneeharless.com

Acknowledgements

I have so much thanks for the readers that requested more of Carson. I love this town just as much as the rest of you.

I can't even begin these acknowledgements without mentioning Patricia, Lisa, Amanda R., Sally, Crystal, Amanda A, and Kelli. You all waited patiently for me to deliver this story to you and made sure that I wouldn't miss any deadlines. Patricia, if it wasn't for you this book probably wouldn't have happened.

My family: you all make everything worth it. Thank you for allowing me to follow my dreams and be the best writer that I can. I love you all so much.

To my readers: Welcome back to Carson. I hope that the wait has been worth it and you're ready for many years to come of Carson shenanigans.

About the Author

Renee Harless is a romance writer with an affinity for wine and a passion for telling a good story.

Renee Harless, her husband, and children live in Blue Ridge Mountains of Virginia. She studied Communication, specifically Public Relations, at Radford University.

Growing up, Renee always found a way to pursue her creativity. It began by watching endless runs of White Christmas- yes even in the summer – and learning every word and dance from the movie. She could still sing "Sister Sister" if requested. In high school, she joined the show choir and a community theatre group, The Troubadours. After marrying the man of her dreams and moving from her hometown she sought out a different artistic outlet – writing.

To say that Renee is a romance addict would be an understatement. When she isn't chasing her kids around the house, working her day job, or writing, she jumps head first into a romance novel.

Made in the USA
Middletown, DE
14 January 2022